THE
ANCIENT
CHRONICLES

THE
NEWBORN

A NOVEL BY

RICHARD A.
DELGADO

ISBN: 978-1-4834-8392-4 (sc)
ISBN: 978-1-4834-8393-1 (e)

Library of Congress Control Number: 2018908302

Interior Images by Richard A. Delgado.
Author Photo by Yasmine Kateb.

Lulu Publishing Services rev. date: 7/26/2018

With grateful love and appreciation,

To my wife and family, and to everyone else who is reading this book.

ttsburgh

Romulus' Castle

Village

Dark Cave

ALLEGHENY RIVER

Church

soleum

MONONGAHELA RIVER

I

Autumn 1774
Pittsburgh, Pennsylvania

As the autumn season rapidly approached and the dense colors of the sun peeked through the trees, the sunlight spread over a vast area of land that belonged to the Le' Muerte family. The owner of this land was a forty-three-year-old farmer and family man. Marco Le' Muerte was an average looking man with a naturally built physique. He was dedicated to his life's work, and like many men, he worked hard to bring food to his family's table. That morning, Marco decided he wanted to make an elegant dinner for his beautiful and loving wife, Joyce, because it was her thirty-sixth birthday. Marco was a well-known landlord and respected by many in the town, who saw his effort in taking care of his land.

Marco's father had traveled from France to the new world at the age of twenty and married Marco's mother, a beautiful Englishwoman. Years later, they moved to the town of Pittsburgh, where Marco was born. Despite the couple's several attempts to have more children, Marco was their only child. Marco's father raised him to become a strong workingman and to take care of the land and his future family. After the death of his parents from a plague, Marco became even more of his father's son. The older he became, the more he grew into the strict and committed mind-set of how things should be done. Always remembering his parents' teachings, he did what he had to do every day to bring honor to his parents and family.

On the Le' Muerte's property, a curious ten-year-old boy named Leonardo played hide-and-seek in the woods with his friend Simon, who was seven. Simon had an older brother, David, who'd recently turned twelve. David and Simon were two African boys, the children of Chloe Jaddea, who worked as a servant for the Le' Muertes. Marco had saved Chloe and her children when they were almost killed during a slave trade in the city's town square five years ago. Ever since, they had worked for the family in gratitude for saving their lives. Marco and Joyce never intended to have slaves. To them, owning another person seemed inhumane. Throughout the years, they became fond of Chloe and her sons, and were treated like family. This humble way of thinking created controversy within the town for the Le' Muertes. Being judged and seen as unwelcomed members of the community was the last thing Marco wanted for his family. He was the black sheep of his family and even within townspeople, because of his beliefs. Though, in spite of it all, the one person that kept his feet on the ground was Joyce's love and humility towards others.

Back at the Le' Muerte house, their only daughter, a beautiful and angelic thirteen-year-old named Alydia, helped her mother prep for dinner by stripping ears of corn they had grown. Many told Alydia that she was the spitting image of her mother, to the exact point of her deep blue eyes. Alydia was at the age of learning how to cook and clean. She was learning how to cook from her mother and how to clean from Chloe. It was custom for young girls to learn how to cook and clean to become good wives and mothers for their future husbands and children.

"Where on earth is your father?" Joyce asked Alydia with a concerned look.

"Perhaps Papa went for a walk in the woods to check on the land."

"But why would your father go out in the woods when he knows how dangerous it can get when the sun starts to set? Your father always makes me worry about him."

"But you know Papa loves you," said Alydia, happiness gleaming in her eyes.

"I know he does, sweetheart. That is something I will always know." Joyce smiled warmly.

As Joyce and Alydia stripped the last few ears of corn, Joyce was curious about what Marco was doing. Hours passed as she cooked and cleaned, trying to rid her mind of worry about her husband's absence. However, cooking and cleaning did not help. Joyce went through all the rooms of the house. She even searched for him in their bedroom, hoping he was asleep there after a long walk in the woods. He was nowhere to be found. She was beginning to feel anxious, hoping nothing tragic had happened to him.

Joyce headed back downstairs to the kitchen. "Chloe?"

"Yes, ma'am?"

"Have you seen my husband around?"

"Sorry, I haven't seen Mr. Le' Muerte, ma'am," Chloe responded as she scrubbed the kitchen floor. "I am sure he will be back in any moment."

"I am so worried about him. His rifle is not here, and he has been gone for hours."

Chloe tried to reassure Joyce. "You should not be worried, because Mr. Le' Muerte is a strong man. Nothing can harm him."

Despite Chloe's generous compliments, Joyce was still worried. She walked to the kitchen window facing the woods, hoping Marco was safe.

After another hour passed, Marco arrived home with a dead rabbit in one hand and his rifle in the other. He left a dead deer lying outside on the front lawn.

"Where in God's name have you been, Marco?" Joyce said. "Do you have any idea how worried I've been, not knowing where you were?"

"I was out hunting for dinner to start the celebration of your birthday."

After hearing what he had been up to for the past several hours, Joyce was so relieved and happy. She ran and hugged and kissed him. He had remembered her birthday. Feeling comforted, Marco asked Joyce to bring the children inside, including Chloe and her two sons, to celebrate.

"Why do you torment me like this Marco, you know how I get when I start to worry," Joyce said. "I am vulnerable without you my love."

"Joyce, didn't I make a vow to God the day we got married, that I will always protect and care for you?" Marco replied. "There is no need to worry every time I leave the house for a few hours."

"Now, don't start making fun of me Marco."

"I am only teasing," Marco chuckled. "I love you."

"I love you too." Joyce said, giving a gentle kiss to Marco.

As the sun started to set and the moon slowly began to form in the beautiful gray sky, Marco, Joyce, Chloe, and the children sat around the dinner table, enjoying their dinner. Except for Leonardo. He was nowhere to be found. Joyce asked Chloe to call Leonardo to come and eat because it was getting too late to play outside. Marco gave Joyce a stern look. He did not want Leonardo at the table. He wanted Leonardo nowhere in sight during this special celebration.

Alydia, watching her father's expression, became concerned. She did not understand why her father acted that way. She wondered why he did not treat Leonardo with any affection or want him sitting at the table. Alydia was sad at witnessing his spiteful gestures toward her brother, but she kept her thoughts to herself and ate her dinner.

At Joyce's request, Chloe went outside to call Leonardo. He ran inside and headed to the dining room to take a piece of bread from the table. As he reached over to grab the bread, Marco struck his hand off the table. "What is the matter with you?" he yelled at Leonardo. "Do you have no manners at all, Leonardo?"

"But, Papa," Leonardo said with despair in his voice.

"But nothing! Go to your room. You won't be eating dinner tonight, because of your rude manners." Marco snatched the piece of bread from Leonardo and put it on his own plate.

As Leonardo stood there, he felt unwanted and unloved by his father. His eyes began to fill with tears. All he could think of was how much he hated Marco and wished he were not his father. He looked at everyone at the table, one by one, with so much sadness in his heart. Alydia looked at Leonardo with so much sorrow, seeing how her brother was treated. She wanted to speak up, but she couldn't find her voice. Then Leonardo looked to his father again with even more hatred. "I hate you! I hate you!" Leonardo screamed. The words just came out; he screamed at his father, expressing how much hatred he had for him. Then he ran out of the house and into their log cabin outside.

Joyce was heartbroken for Leonardo. She began to argue with Marco. "Why do you act the way you do, and why are you always so cruel to Leonardo? After all, Leonardo is our only son."

"He is not my son!" Marco yelled furiously, as he slammed his fist on the table. "You of all people should know that, Joyce!"

"Marco!"

"He is not my son, and he never will be!"

"How dare you! Don't you ever say that again, Marco Le' Muerte. Leonardo is our only son. We raised him as our own. Try putting yourself in his place, and remember the feeling of once being a child," Joyce said with such disappointment.

"I wasn't raised to be a fool Joyce, nor did I raise this family to act like fools."

Upset, Joyce stood up and headed to the cabin to nurture Leonardo, but the door was locked from the inside. She begged him to let her in, but Leonardo, crying softly in anger, wanted to be left alone. Joyce tried to comfort him, telling him how much everyone loved and cared for him.

"Sweetheart, I am sorry for the actions of your father. You must remember that we love you very much. Alydia loves you, I love you, and I know it's very hard to see it, but even your father loves you too. Please come back inside the house, we are here for you Leonardo."

After a while of persuasion and silence, Joyce, still worried, decided to go back inside the house. She reminded herself that Leonardo would feel better by the morning.

It wasn't the first time this had happened. About a month ago, Leonardo tried to run away after receiving a terrible whipping for disobeying Marco. It was a heartbreaking experience for Joyce to witness, as the boy she raised be beaten and then go missing for days in the woods. Leonardo always managed to find his way back home and did his best to continue on his life as if nothing ever happened. Regardless of whether her son was blood-related, Joyce knew in her heart that there was something special within Leonardo.

As Joyce walked back to the house, all she could think of was giving him the space he needed.

"Mama, will Leonardo be okay?" Alydia asked.

"Yes, my dear. Give him some time, I am sure he will be fine in the morning."

Alydia gave a doubtful look, because she knew how her father's words always hurt Leonardo. "He will be okay, I promise," Joyce reassured her daughter.

As night fell upon the land, Leonardo's emotions started to subside, but anger and hatred lingered within him. He was distraught by how everyone acted, except his sister. He could never stay mad at her, because he truly cared for her. Overwhelmed with emotions, he fell into a deep sleep and let his dreams take him elsewhere.

Deep into the night, black crows began to fly over the cabin. Packs of wolves could be heard in the distance, howling, growling, fighting amongst themselves. Lightning and thunder began to be seen and heard over the town, as if a huge thunderstorm was underway. Cold winds began to breeze through the land, making the branches of the trees sway within the current. Evil lurked in his dreams and upon his family. He dreamed they were attacked by a dark entity that affected everything in its path, like a plague. There were screams of pain and suffering from the darkness, and Leonardo desperately wanted to save them. Joyce, Marco, Chloe and her two children were grabbed by supernatural beings, and one by one, Leonardo witnessed them being taken by these monsters into a dark abyss. He tried grabbing hold of Alydia's blood-covered hand. He wanted to pull her out from the darkness, but it was too late; she was gone, and only shadows were left hovering above him. The whole house seemed to shake and rumble, and flames of fire were spreading, engulfing all of his memories into ash. Demon-like laughter echoed around him, and voices were calling his name and telling him that his life was no longer his, that there was no way out, no salvation, and no redemption but only horror that awaited him. There was nothing he could do but accept that his family had been ripped away from him. Cold and scared, Leonardo felt alone in a dark world filled with despair and nothingness.

The next morning, Leonardo woke up from a cold breeze seeping through the cabin. He felt lonely and was saddened from the dream, but mostly he felt a feeling of emptiness, for a reason he could not explain. He got up from the hay he had laid out to sleep on and started heading to the house. He felt that there was something not right. As he walked into the house, the smell of death was in the air; it felt as if it had been deserted for years. Leonardo cautiously began to walk through the house with a sudden fear running through his body. The entire house was in chaos: chairs had been thrown across the rooms, plates shattered; most of the windows were broken; and, worst of all, the smell of blood permeated the house. This was not a scene for an innocent child to have to witness. Leonardo went around the house calling for his family, even though it seemed obvious that someone or something had come uninvited in the middle of the night and destroyed everything. Unexpectedly, he found David lying face down on the floor in one of the upstairs rooms; he was dead and covered in blood. Leonardo ran out into the hallway, trembling and frightened of what could have happened to the others. Blood was splattered all over the floors and the walls; he could not comprehend what had happened last night or who could have done something so horrific to his family.

When Leonardo got to his parents' bedroom, he found his mother and father lying dead on the floor at the foot of the bed. They were covered with their own blood; their hands were over their necks as if they were blocking themselves from being attacked from some type of animal. As he cried and cried, he tried to move them to see if they would wake up, but it was too late. Leonardo screamed for his mother to wake up; he loved her so much and was not ready for her to leave him yet. He even screamed for his father to wake up, despite how cruel he had been toward him the night before. He finally came to the realization that his parents were dead and that there was nothing he could do to bring them back to life. Leonardo's eyes were filled with tears as he started to give up. Then he realized that he had to find Alydia, Chloe, and Simon. He looked throughout the house, but they were nowhere to be found. As the feeling of loss and fear became great and heartbreaking, Leonardo had no other option but to run away. His nightmare became a reality, and there was no way out. He ran and ran as fast as he could, crying and shouting in sadness, vowing to himself that he would never return.

Leonardo managed to stay hidden in the woods for seven days. He wandered around, desperately looking for any place to go, any place that would take him away from all his suffering. The few houses that he stumbled upon refused to help him as he sought refuge. Remembering the moments of feeling the warmth of his own bed and knowing that he had food every night. Hunger became unbearable as the hours passed; the only way he could calm his hunger was by eating small insects and quenching his thirst by drinking out of small ponds of water that he found along his path. Every night, Leonardo felt the sharp pain of the cold that came through the woods, as only the clothes on his back kept him warm. Nevertheless, during those nights, he would look up at the sky, and the stars would remind him of the days when he was truly happy with his family, when there was laughter and everyone got along. Memories of listening to his mother's bed time stories, Alydia smiling and carefree, playing with him on the porch, and playing ball with Simon and David every morning during the summer and enjoying the delicious food that Chloe would serve them during the day. Yet, of all these memories, Leonardo remembered Alydia's smile the most. He missed the days how she would hug him anytime she had the chance. There was simply no other safer place to be than in her arms. Yet the more he remembered, the more the darkness would push through and remind him that everyone he loved and cared about was dead. Leonardo was living in fear not only from the events of that day but also from the creatures lurking around the woods, ready to hunt for anything to feed on. Every night, he mourned and cried for his family, even though he knew that there was nothing he could do to bring them back.

It had been a week since his family was mysteriously massacred. All was quiet that morning as Leonardo hid inside a hollow log. Suddenly he heard movement in the woods; he got out of the log to find out where the noise was coming from. An old man by the name of Wilber Hatchet was crossing through the woods with his wagon, right by where Leonardo was standing. Startled by seeing a little boy stranded in the middle of the woods, Wilber stopped his horse and got off his wagon, raising both hands to show that he meant no harm to Leonardo.

"This is no place for a small boy to be, especially in these parts of the woods," Wilber said with concern. "God only knows what you have been through and what kind of dangerous beasts and wild creatures are lurking about."

Leonardo was desperate, and this man showed him no harm. His only desire at this moment was to leave the woods.

"Please, sir, take me with you," Leonardo begged the man.

Wilber felt pity for the poor boy; he thought of what he would do if it were his grandchild or one of his own children.

"What is your name, boy?

"Leonardo."

"Just Leonardo?" he asked curiously, wondering what happened to the boy.

"Just Leonardo, sir." Leonardo replied, as he lowered his head in sorrow. He did not want to say his last name because it was his family's name, and his family no longer existed.

The old man, with all his strength, picked up Leonardo and set him on the back of his wagon, where he kept his work tools. Wilber noticed how hungry and thirsty the boy was; he reached over and grabbed the last loaf of bread he had, along with his container that was filled with fresh water and gave them to Leonardo. "You must be really hungry and thirsty," Wilber said, "Don't you worry my boy, we will be out of these woods in no time," Wilber sat back on his horse and continued his journey.

They rode through the woods for the rest of the day, taking various inward and outward turns, avoiding boulders and traps that were set for the wild animals. Leonardo, sitting in the back of the wagon, felt comforted, not only from the food he had eaten but also from the feeling of finally being safe. He kept to himself throughout the ride, observing the woods around him until they finally reached town. "We are finally here" Wilber said. Leonardo looked over to him and asked, "Where are we?" Wilber gave a chuckle and replied, "This my boy, is the town of Pittsburgh. The town of possibilities." The town of Pittsburgh was filled with great color and life. There were people all around, from humble farmers to hard workingmen. It was occupied with high-class people, such as politicians, landowners, bankers, and those who came from royalty. However, not all was what it seemed in this town. There were also people who craved money and power, such as prostitutes and thieves. The population also included the poor children and families with no homes who sought mercy and support from the wealthy to survive.

Further into town, Wilber stopped his wagon at an old blacksmith forge. He looked over at Leonardo and told him to stay in the wagon until he came back from taking care of some personal business. Leonardo sat at the back of the wagon, waiting patiently for him to return, but as minutes passed, he began to feel uncomfortable with the townspeople staring at him like he was an outcast. At least half an hour went by, and finally Wilber came back with a man known as Thomas Hill. He was a tall man, with short hair that was combed to the side, and fine thin mustache. Wilber and Thomas whispered to each other as they stood next to the forge. Leonardo tried to eavesdrop and then realized that the old man was trying to sell him away. Thomas made his fortune by buying and selling homeless children to other families as slaves. Realizing this, Leonardo quickly jumped off the wagon and ran through the town, trying to find a place to hide. He found an open alleyway and hid behind the street trash. Trying to catch his breath, Leonardo thought about how much he had been through. He made a promise to himself that one day he would have revenge on whoever was responsible for all of this and his family's death.

II

Days turned to weeks and then into months. Leonardo managed to settle into the town by living on the streets, but he was alone. From the cause of hunger, he had become a thief who stole food and money from the rich and the poor. He also managed to escape multiple times the merchants who tried to kill him for stealing. As clever as he was, all that ended when he was caught and captured by a group of town officers. Leonardo stood in court in front of the town judge, and instead of being sentenced to prison, he was to be taken to a slave trade in order to pay back his debt to the town for stealing. He was sent to Le Fleur, a small slave trade on the far side of town, owned by none other than the reaper of children, Thomas Hill. Leonardo remembered how Thomas tried to take him months ago to be his slave. Now, it seemed that Thomas finally got his way.

As Leonardo entered the slave trade, he learned that life was rough, no matter how old a person was. The old and the young were shipped off to different places to serve the wealthy. The older slaves would be responsible for cleaning and cooking. The younger slaves would be responsible for the upkeep of the farm and the land. La Fleur, however, was known for receiving young slaves, and the younger they were, the better.

The small land where Thomas kept his slaves was filled with pain and despair, and many if not most of the slaves were severely beaten and treated like wild animals. Those who were there the longest were forced into hard labor, and those who were young and healthy did the easy work until they were forced into the work that the old and weary were unable to do. The most painful to watch were the slaves who could not work or who were barely able to stand on their own two feet. Without hesitation, Thomas would punish them; either by lashing them against the old oak tree or have them shot in the back of their head. Very rarely though, for severe punishments, he would have his wild dogs kill and tear into the slaves, for his own amusement. Thomas was truly an unsettling man, with a very cruel sense of humor.

The first night within the slave trade, Leonardo was put in the underground cellar where they were kept in groups of twelve. It was difficult for Leonardo to get any sleep, as he could hear gunshots being fired above. Leonardo covered his ears in fear. He could not understand what was going on as he heard the footsteps of the armed men of Le Fleur who were yelling in anger.

Hearing Thomas shout, "Get them, you fools! Don't let them escape!" the other slaves in the cellar knew to keep to themselves and stay quiet, as they had been taught by the other slaves who were there before them. As the shouting and gunshots continued, Leonardo realized from the yelling that three slaves had escaped but then were shot down. As the armed men were laughing and making jokes about the slaves, Thomas's footsteps approached the cellar. He yelled down for all the slaves to hear, "Ladies and gentlemen, hear me well! If any of you run away or try to escape—" he took his gun from his holster and shot one of the slaves right between the eyes— "this will happen." As Thomas ordered the men to take away the dead bodies to be fed to his wild dogs, he walked toward Leonardo's cellar. He said, smiling, "Your one-way ticket to high heaven, boy."

Leonardo realized there was no way to escape and that he was now alone. As reality began to sink in, he suddenly noticed two strange kids in the cell next to his. They were siblings, a boy and a girl; the boy seemed to be the same age as he was, while the girl was older, around the age of twelve or thirteen. What caught Leonardo's attention was that they were staring straight at him, and they didn't seem bothered by what had just happened. Both appeared calm but alert. They both kept silent, and within the chaos, kept close as they held each other's hands. While Leonardo kept looking back at them, as he himself was trembling, he noticed their white, pale skin and their sharp nails. Most unique about them was their hollow, dead eyes. He knew better than to involve himself with strangers. Feeling troubled and knowing that there was no hope, he slowly backed into the corner. His sadness was blanketed by the hope that one day he would find his sister, Alydia, and the happiness that he once felt would come back into his life.

Time continued, and Leonardo knew nothing of the outside world. Strangely enough though, the two strange siblings that he once saw in that horrifying night of death were long gone without a trace, as if they never existed. If only he had been able to escape with them, Leonardo believed that he would be in a better place than this. The nineteen-year-old boy living in Le Fleur, forced into hard labor, was losing hope and the will to fight for his freedom. Eventually, a very wealthy landlord of the town by the name of Matthew Cooper bought him from the slave trade and took Leonardo to his land, that was set a couple of hours away from Pittsburgh. Mr. Cooper was known to buy slaves to work on his land and then work them so hard they either got too old to work, died from too much work, or were killed for disobeying him. He was a short and plump man who always carried a staff with him to help with his injured knee from the war. He had been a landlord for the past fifty-two years and had recently become the chairman of an upcoming crop-growing company for the town.

Leonardo was becoming a man; he had a slim body with dark brown hair that almost reached his shoulders, and the clothes that he wore had been given to him by a previous slave that worked at Le Fleur. When Mr. Cooper bought Leonardo, he knew in his heart that none of his hard work that he went through for the past nine years at Le Fleur would matter. Leonardo remembered the conversation when Mr. Cooper bought him, where he realized the ugly truth behind the slave trade. In spite of his respected military background, he was very good in hiding his true motives and intentions from everyone.

"Why did you choose to buy me, sir?" Leonardo asked.

"Because I need a young slave to continue the work, the work that my other slaves could not finish before their passing."

"What happened to them, sir?"

"I shot them, each one of them, for disobeying me or for being too old to continue the work," Mr. Cooper answered.

Mr. Cooper told him what his chores and responsibilities were; he would start at sunrise and finish before dark. He explained the rules of what to do and what not to do. The most important tasks were to make sure that the cattle were safe from the wolves during the day and night, and to maintain the crops for his growing crop business. If Leonardo failed to follow any of the rules and tasks, Mr. Cooper made it clear that he would not hesitate to punish him or kill him.

Days went on, and the life of a slave was Leonardo's reality. His feelings for his family and his tragic childhood memories were gradually fading away, and it only seemed that his life had only gotten worse. Having faith held no value, and his future had no meaning anymore. Life became worthless, and in that moment, Leonardo thought of when he was a boy, how he dreamt of becoming someone with great importance. What affected him the most was the sorrow and anger in his heart that had started to fade. His feelings had once encouraged the chance of seeking revenge.

Leonardo began to get used to his life as a working slave. As he got older and matured, he realized that he was not treated as a human being; he had become an instrument for any wealthy citizen to use. In spite of how things turned out for Leonardo, he managed to learn various skills. He learned how to feed farm animals, hunt for food, and craft useful tools out of wood. Leonardo became knowledgeable of the land and knew his way around; sometimes he felt that he knew it better than Mr. Cooper did. At times, Leonardo felt blessed to have a place to call home, but at other times, he referred to it as hell, because of Mr. Cooper's lack of appreciation for the work he had done. There were days when, without reason, Mr. Cooper would punish Leonardo by lashing him with a whip. There were times when Mr. Cooper would punish him, just depending on his mood or whether if he was drinking that day of. Somedays there was simply no mercy in his punishments.

Throughout all the hardships that were faced each day, Leonardo felt like someone was always watching him in the shadows, observing him day in and day out. Most of the nights, he felt scared of the creatures lurking around the land. This was a fear that had crept up on Leonardo, a fear he could not describe; all he knew was that he sensed danger.

✻   ✻   ✻   ✻

Back in the woods, an evil, dark, and mysterious entity had been watching Leonardo carefully, waiting for the opportune moment to take him away from his horrible life.

III

Half a decade had passed, and Leonardo was a twenty-five-year-old man. He had changed from being a young teenage boy to a six-foot-tall man with a strong physique. Every day, Leonardo put his strongest effort into his work, so that one day he could receive his freedom from Mr. Cooper. Some days seemed too difficult to get through, because of the harsh punishments from Mr. Cooper, and it seemed almost impossible for Leonardo to reach his freedom.

At Mr. Cooper's house, Leonardo was bringing firewood for the fireplace for Mr. Cooper and his arriving guests. As Leonardo was headed inside to place the wood in the chimney, he noticed, while walking past one of the back windows, who the guests were. There was Madam Elizabeth Williams and Sir Michael Hewitt, both part of the crop-growing business. Elizabeth was a twenty-year-old woman who had beautiful blue eyes and soft, pale skin. Everyone knew her to be kind, smart, and gentle, but she also was able to show an attitude to those who deserved it and to anyone who defied the laws. Her cousin Michael was a thirty-year-old man. He was short but had handsome features yet was a man who had no compassion or remorse. He had worked as an attorney for a few years before getting into politics. Both were among the most respected individuals in the entire town.

What really caught Leonardo's eye was what they were wearing: rich, silk jackets, shiny new shoes, and the most fascinating was the silver staff Mr. Hewitt had in his possession. Truly a man of power and greatness, so he thought. Leonardo wished that one day he would be able to live the life of a rich man and have a beautiful young woman at his side, such as Ms. Williams. Something about her made him feel attracted. Through out his years in the slave trade and working for Mr. Cooper, had he ever seen such a beautiful and elegant woman.

Ms. Williams caught Leonardo's eye at the window, and she gave a sweet smile as a kind gesture. Mr. Cooper caught her gaze; he turned toward the window to see who or what she was looking at, but by when he turned to look at the window, Leonardo was gone. However, Mr. Cooper knew that it was Leonardo who had been standing at the window. He looked back at Ms. Williams and felt jealous; she was a beautiful young woman and should not be interested in a slave like Leonardo, it was certainly the last thing he needed.

"You should not pay any attention to him, Elizabeth. He is a worthless thing with no knowledge of anything," said Mr. Cooper.

"But he is like anyone else. He is just a human being," Elizabeth responded.

"Leonardo is a pitiful parasite who has no emotions or feelings. He walks around like a lifeless soul, doing what I demand him to do. He is a slave, my dear Elizabeth; he is not like anyone else," explained Mr. Cooper, trying to control his temper. "Now, I would be pleased if we could return to our proper conversation about our crop business."

For the rest of the evening, they sipped their warm tea and continued talking about how they were going to increase their sales and make more money.

Outside, after Leonardo left the house, he went to the stables to check on Timber. Timber was a gentle and smart horse. His entire coat was of a dark brown shade, except for his four legs, where each leg seemed to have been dipped in white paint. Timber belonged to Mr. Cooper, but Leonardo was the one who raised him and cared for him. While Leonardo was brushing Timber's coat and telling him about what his future would be like if he were a rich man, he saw Mr. Hewitt and Ms. Williams leaving the house and getting into their carriage.

"Thank you for coming. We shall meet again next month to talk about any changes in the plantation," Mr. Cooper said to his guests.

"Most certainly. It was a pleasure Mr. Cooper, thank you for having us over this evening," Mr. Hewitt said. "I'll be forwarding our new arrangements to the town's council soon enough."

"Time is gold Michael. Let's make sure we don't make it go to waste," Mr. Cooper stated.

"Would you please tell Leonardo that he is doing a wonderful job maintaining your land?" Elizabeth asked Mr. Cooper.

"Of course," Mr. Cooper replied, knowing well enough that he would not pass the message along.

"Thank you. After all, if it wasn't for him, God only knows what would have become of your land."

"Are you trying to tell me that I don't take care for my land? That I am a lazy man? If that is the case, Elizabeth, then you have no idea what I am capable of doing."

"All I am trying to say, Matthew, is that you should value what you have before it's too late," Ms. Williams explained.

"How dare you! I demand you leave at once, unless you want to see your precious slave beaten to death!"

"You are nothing but an old, ill-mannered man who can't see past the tip of his nose!"

Ms. Williams and Mr. Cooper exchanged a long, hard stare before she shut the door to their carriage.

Mr. Hewitt apologized to Mr. Cooper for Elizabeth's rude behavior and made sure that business was still set in motion between them before taking the path back home.

"Elizabeth, we do business with this man. Why would you get involved in his personal affairs?" Mr. Hewitt asked, aggravated with her.

"Michael, you know well enough all he really cares about is himself and his wealth. I promise you, sooner or later something horrible will come upon him."

"That's enough, Elizabeth!"

Elizabeth was not sorry, but she apologized to Mr. Hewitt and gazed out into the woods for the remainder of the ride. There was only one image that came into her thoughts, and that was of Leonardo's gentle and captivating eyes. It had been a while that another man's eyes captured her heart in such a way. She wondered if she would ever see him again in the near future.

As soon as they left, Mr. Cooper yelled out to Leonardo to bring more wood for the fireplace. Once Leonardo finished feeding Timber and brushing his coat, he headed out to chop more wood for his master. It took him twenty minutes to gather the amount of wood Mr. Cooper wanted. He walked into the house to set the wood inside the fireplace, when suddenly Mr. Cooper charged at him with his staff. He hit him across the back, making Leonardo stumble onto the floor in agonizing pain. Mr. Cooper was infuriated with Leonardo and wanted to kill him. His anger and frustration ran through his body and drove him to beat Leonardo. He hated the way Elizabeth had looked at Leonardo, and he was disgusted by her compliment towards him. Most of all, he despised how much she had an affection for slaves.

"Get up! Get up, you worthless piece of trash!" Sir Cooper yelled at Leonardo. "I said get up now!"

Leonardo was in pain, but he knew that he had to obey no matter what. His pain and hatred made him want to defend himself, but his desire to stay alive overpowered his emotions. He got up again, and turning to Mr. Cooper, he could see how the madness had corrupted within his eyes.

"That's more like it! Stand up like a real man!"

Mr. Cooper grabbed Leonardo by the throat and punched him as hard as he could, until Leonardo did not have the strength to move anymore. Mr. Cooper did not care about Leonardo's blood being spilled everywhere. He threw him against the wall and held him down against the floor, punching and beating Leonardo until all his anger flared out. Leonardo knew he could not defend himself no matter how much pain he was enduring. Even then, with all his strength, he was trying to withstand the beatings. Unfortunately, Mr. Cooper realized that Leonardo was able to get through the pain, so he grabbed his staff again and swung it across the back of his head. This time, the pain was unbearable; Leonardo tumbled back and fell to the ground unconscious. Mr. Cooper stood in front of him, holding his staff and feeling much better now that the anger was out of his system.

"That should put you in your place," he said, pleased with himself yet exhausted. "Damn that woman, telling me that I am not capable of maintaining my land."

Two hours passed, and Leonardo finally woke up. Pain spread throughout his body; he looked around and discovered that he had been thrown outside. He went over to a small pond nearby and washed the blood from his face. Leonardo felt a long cut on his left cheek, from Mr. Cooper's cane, and he knew it would be a permanent reminder of his pain. It was getting too dark for him to be out at night. Knowing well enough, that regardless what he just went through tonight, he needed to rest so that he could continue his chores early in the morning. There would be no moment of mercy for him. He dragged himself to the small log cabin where he lived. It was located yards behind Mr. Cooper's house. Once inside, he suddenly heard Timber cry out in panic. Ignoring his injured body, Leonardo quickly went out to keep Timber quiet, but as he tried to calm him down, Timber seemed to panic more. He seemed to have sensed an unwelcomed visitor lurking around the stables. Leonardo had no idea what was causing him to act out in such fear, but after a few calming whispers and reassurances that there was nothing there, Timber finally calmed down.

Leonardo returned to his cabin, when suddenly he realized he had left his tools out in the woods earlier that day. Knowing that Mr. Cooper would punish him again for not having his tools with him when doing his chores, Leonardo decided to go out and search for them before his body gave out from the pain. Leonardo used all the strength he had left and began to search near the woods. Minutes passed before he finally found his tools near a tree stump. As he was reaching over to pick them up, he became aware of a dark figure standing in front of him. He looked up and saw a man with a slim figure; he had long raven black hair that reached his shoulders. He was as pale as the moon but had dark emerald eyes that were as empty as the ocean. Leonardo felt a strange sense of lust surrounding the man who was standing in the shadows of the woods.

"Who are you?" Leonardo asked as he stood up to get a better look at the man.

The strange man did not answer; he simply stood there staring down at Leonardo. Again, Leonardo asked for his name because he was intruding on the land. The man gracefully gave a sly smile as if he was up to something. As the strange man continued to stare at him, Leonardo began to study this mysterious man. He did not look like an ordinary aristocrat. The clothes he wore seemed to be made from extravagant silks. He was wearing a suede black cloak, and underneath he wore a hand-sewn embroidered waistcoat with a green silk jabot that matched his eyes. His shoes were of the highest quality that Leonardo had ever seen. Undoubtedly, Leonardo knew that this man was not from the town, or any place near. He knew this man was no ordinary man, and the way he dressed seemed too old for this time period.

"What is your name, sir?" Leonardo asked again.

The man just stood there.

Leonardo was beginning to feel frustrated at the man for not answering his questions. The strange man kept staring at Leonardo, as if he had known him for years. Finally, the man spoke with a voice that captured Leonardo's soul.

"Is this your land?" the strange man asked.

"This land is the property of Sir Matthew Cooper."

"It is a very beautiful piece of property. It is such a shame that his heart does not value the beauty of it. Like the way your heart does, Leonardo."

Leonardo felt confused. How did this man, whom he had never met before, know his name?

"I've been watching you for some time now, Leonardo. You have no idea how much I've been waiting for this moment."

"Please, sir, tell me who you are. What do you want from me?" asked Leonardo.

"What do I want?" the man asked. "What do I want, Leonardo?" he repeated as he looked at Leonardo with a great craving in his mysterious green eyes.

As the man said those words, Leonardo began to slowly back away; he could feel this man was dangerous. The clothes that he wore and his accent that he carried, was from a different world, a much darker world. Moreover, this man had been watching Leonardo for days.

Leonardo was able to get a better look at the man as he came into the moonlight. He saw that the man had long, sharp nails and, looking closer, he had a pair of sharp teeth like a canine. A cold shiver made the hairs of his neck rise. The sense of death began to sore over him, and his heart began to pound faster and faster. His hands began to slowly tremble and his eyes widened. Quickly his instincts of survival began to manifest and he felt that his life was in grave danger. Frightened of the man, he immediately started running back to his cabin. However, the man was too quick for Leonardo. He appeared in front of him with a silent speed that no human could see with the naked eye.

"What are you afraid of? You've been through worse," the man said, as if he knew everything about Leonardo's life. In a flash, the man grabbed Leonardo's neck and sank his teeth into the pulsing vein that beat through his neck. An immediate pain had spread through Leonardo's body, a pain that no human has ever experienced before. Leonardo was defenseless against the man's strength. He tried to push him away, but it was too late; the man was taking Leonardo's life.

Memories of his early life became visible as each drop of blood was sucked out of him. Leonardo felt a mix of emotions: pleasure, pain, weakness, and strength. As he was remembering his life, Leonardo was in agonizing pain. He tried to push the man away, but his body was weak and lifeless. What seemed like hours passed, and the man finally let Leonardo go. Leonardo fell to the ground, barely alive and vulnerable. Blood trickled from the man's lips and dripped off his chin; he felt fully satisfied now that he was finally able to feed on Leonardo.

"I have taken most of your life's soul, my friend, so close to death, but do not be afraid. Soon you will feel no more pain and suffering," he whispered, kneeling next to Leonardo.

"No!" Leonardo cried out. "Please, sir, I cannot die like this. I cannot leave this world with my heart filled with vengeance. Help me please!" Leonardo was in great pain as he saw flashbacks of his dead family.

The man knew how it felt to seek vengeance as he looked into Leonardo's agonizing eyes. He remembered that he himself was once a mortal man living in London, thirsty for revenge. The memory of his beloved wife, Hannah, came to mind. He remembered the day when he witnessed the death of his wife right in front of him. She had been raped and murdered by a group of men who called themselves Marcheurs de Nuit, the Nightwalkers. A few years after that night, he was turned to a creature with great power and strength. With his newfound power, he was able to get his revenge on the men who killed his wife. Even then, hearing Hannah's screams and her agonizing pain upset his thoughts. In spite of that horrific moment nearly four hundred years ago, the man still mourned her death each day.

He pitied Leonardo; his heart was heavy with loss, and he had a need for justice. The man also knew that those emotions would make Leonardo become an extraordinary creature. Thinking of the possibility of turning Leonardo, he knew it would take time and patience to teach him everything. Nevertheless, he knew that Leonardo would fill the void that was once shared with his maker. Most of all, he knew that together they would become glorious immortals.

As Leonardo was lying on the ground unconscious, the man knew he would not give Leonardo a choice, because he had never been given a choice himself from his maker. The man knew what had to be done.

He got down near Leonardo, and bringing his arm up to his mouth, tore across his wrist with his canine teeth, letting the blood come undone. Like pouring wine into a glass, the man held up Leonardo's head and poured his blood between his lips. Leonardo's eyes gradually opened as the blood coursed down his throat. His breathing began to get heavy, and his heartbeat began to race. The blood was now flowing through Leonardo's body, invading his mortal soul and replacing it with a new immortal life. As minutes passed, every part of Leonardo that was once human washed away into pain, and his ambition for justice began to take form.

"This, my friend, shall give you eternal life. A life you have never imagined," the strange man said as he gave his blood to Leonardo to feed on.

Death was waiting at his doorstep, seeking his last human breath. Leonardo began to feel the pain subsiding, and his breathing was coming down to a slow rhythm. He looked at the man's face as he slowly pulled away from his wrist; suddenly his heart began to beat slower and slower until it stopped beating. There was no more pain. For the first time in his life, Leonardo felt peace. It seemed that death took hours to come over Leonardo's body; black crows began to fly over him, wolves howled in the distance, and the spirit of the trees witnessed his body dying. Finally, Leonardo opened his eyes. He felt confused as he looked around for the stranger, who was nowhere to be found. Leonardo felt ill, but with all his strength, he crawled back to his cabin to be away from the darkness. He could feel an unbearable pain in his stomach, and an overwhelming pressure on his chest. As if his heart and lungs were being crushed by an incredible force, making it hard for him breath. Noticing the animals' strange behavior, Leonardo forced himself to get up and run. He ran all the way to the cabin without looking back. Once in, he shut the door, and all was quiet again. Leaning against the shut door, Leonardo noticed he was covered in blood. Unfortunately, he was able to remember only fragments of what happened to him back in the woods.

After waiting for a few minutes to pass, Leonardo went outside to the small pond behind the cabin. He pulled his shirt over his head and started washing the blood from his clothes and body. After trying his best to wash away the blood, he quietly went back to his cabin to get some much-needed peace and quiet. However, it seemed that he would never get that peace and quiet after all.

A sharp, throbbing pain began to form in his neck, and his insides felt like they were on fire. Leonardo started to remember everything that had happened in the woods. From all the pain and exhaustion, he fell to the ground headfirst and became unconscious.

The next morning, Leonardo woke up and started to prepare for a new day of work. It seemed that last night's incident did not occur to Leonardo. He put on his working clothes and gathered his supplies to start his chores of cutting the cornfields and getting more wood for Mr. Cooper's house. Suddenly, a wave of nausea swept over Leonardo, and he realized something was not right with him. He felt confused and weak; a pain ran through his body. Leonardo tried not to think too much into it; the pain was just from overworking and lack of sleep. Ignoring the pain, he stepped out of the cabin, but with the sun shining on him, the pain worsened. Again, Leonardo ignored it and continued to the cornfield.

As Leonardo was preparing his tools to gather corn, he began to wonder what happened to him last night and who the mysterious man he had encountered was. He could not forget the moment when death was lingering and he was fighting for life—when blood was given for life and memories of the past were shared.

Realizing that he had a long day ahead of him, Leonardo started to cut the corn for Mr. Cooper's dinner. As the day went on, Leonardo's pain grew stronger, and he had to stop every half hour to regain his strength. He went to the pond and filled his canteen with water; he drank until the pain subsided. The more he tried to regain his strength and drink water, the weaker his body became. What was strange to Leonardo was that the weaker his body became, the more his senses heightened. He could hear animals from inside the woods, walking and eating, and he could hear voices of people from across the town that were miles away. In the midst of his weakness, he could see the stars and the heavens above him more clearly and beautiful than ever before. Feeling the overwhelming magnitude of the sky bearing down on him, the world around him began to change as he looked around. Silent whispers swept through the ground and woods, and the animals slowly began to call out to the light of the sun. His senses were getting so high that even insects could be heard around him, and swift melodies that were created by mother nature herself. Extraordinary sounds that no Human could possibly hear.

What is going on with me?

Leonardo tried to hurry to finish his chores, but the evening was quickly approaching, and Mr. Cooper arrived back at the house with his friend, Thomas Downey. Leonardo stood by holding his cutting tools, prepared to see if Mr. Cooper needed anything, but Mr. Cooper stopped at the doorway of his house, glared at him, walked inside, and closed the door behind him. Again, the pain came upon Leonardo and started to spread like flames in a forest. The pain started from the tips of his fingers and moved through to the core of his body. Leonardo looked at his hands, trying to see what was causing the pain, but nothing could be seen. He started rubbing his hands to relieve the pain, but it only made it worse. He took a closer look and realized that his fingernails had grown half an inch longer and had formed the shape of sharp animal like claws. Leonardo's skin began to burn all over. He drenched himself with water, but that only resulted in his skin turning red and the burning getting worse, as if he was being burned alive. Leonardo, panicked and afraid, ran quickly to his cabin. Once inside, he took off all his clothes to see the damage done to his body. Instead, he saw the redness starting to fade away. Confused and afraid, Leonardo tried to think of a reason for all this madness. He took several long breaths to get rid of the fear that overwhelmed him. Never before in his life had he endured or felt anything like this kind of pain and misery.

Finally, Leonardo's nerves began to settle. He started to pace across the room while observing his newly grown, long, sharp nails. Trying to make sense of everything, he decided to try to go out again, but first he would test the sunlight against his skin. He turned to the cabin window and opened the door. As he was slowly reaching out his hand, a voice inside his head kept telling him to stay in the shade of the cabin, but he ignored it. Leonardo thought this was insane, and he could not understand why his instincts brought a powerful sense of fear about going into the sun. He looked at his hand and then looked outside at the sunlight. If he went back outside again, would the sun burn him alive? Putting aside his fear, he slowly stretched his arm out into the sunlight, and proving his theory correct, the pain started to form again. His hand began to turn red, and his skin started to bubble as smoke ascended from his hand. Leonardo, not able to withstand the pain any longer, quickly snatched his hand back and sought the closest area of shade in the cabin. Leonardo screamed in agony, as the pain grew stronger. He dropped to his knees in mercy, as the pain now spread through his body again. He began to vomit out everything he had in his system. Nothing could help him now.

Hours passed, and the night took over. Inside Mr. Cooper's house, he and Mr. Downey were in the study having a glass of whiskey while discussing the plans for Mr. Cooper's property. When Mr. Cooper realized that Leonardo had not started the fire or that the dinner had not been prepared yet, he went outside and called out to Leonardo, but there was no response. He yelled out again for Leonardo and again received no answer. Mr. Cooper was beginning to feel aggravated.

"Is everything all right, Matthew?" Sir Thomas asked, coming up behind him to see what was going on.

"My slave is being a lazy fool!" he said.

"It seems that he is in his cabin because the light is still on," Mr. Downey said.

"What is that bastard up to now?" Mr. Cooper mumbled under his breath.

Mr. Cooper made his way to Leonardo's house, with Mr. Downey following behind him. He barged into the cabin and walked into Leonardo who was lying on the floor, coughing and spewing out blood. The pain had consumed his entire body. Leonardo could not move; the pain that had overtaken his body had paralyzed him. He could not even acknowledge the fact that Mr. Cooper and his friend had just barged through the door. Leonardo had started to run a fever, the color from his face was gone, and it had seemed as if he had not eaten in months. He felt like he was dying all over again, but this time it was a hundred times worse. Mr. Cooper and Mr. Downey were both disgusted at what they saw.

"For goodness sake!" Having a weak stomach, Mr. Downey walked back outside to breathe in fresh air.

"What's the matter with you? You were fine this morning when I left for town," Mr. Cooper said to Leonardo.

"He must have gotten the plague or some kind of disease that has been spreading around," Mr. Downey yelled from outside the cabin. "You should throw him out before he begins to infect you and everything in your land."

"Pity," Mr. Cooper said without any remorse.

"It's a damn shame how every year these slaves drop like flies. Make sure you throw him out, Matthew, or else things will become complicated for you ... believe me."

"I will take care of it personally, because now I finally have a reason to get rid of this cockroach," Mr. Cooper said, with a look of repulsion on his face.

Once it was decided what to do with Leonardo, Mr. Cooper and Mr. Downey left to go back inside the house. As Mr. Cooper was leaving, he took one last look at Leonardo and thought to himself that he was glad he was going to die; he never had to look at him again. Mr. Downey was quickly getting ready to head back into town, afraid of catching anything Leonardo had. Mr. Downey said his farewells to Mr. Cooper and headed back to town.

Back at Leonardo's cabin, he was struggling to fight the pain and take control of his body, but the illness won over. He was on the floor screaming in agony, as the pain was becoming unbearable. The only thing he could comprehend was that his life was about to end. Leonardo witnessed his skin turning pale white and his veins becoming visible under his skin. Slowly, he began to feel an unbearable coldness spreading across his body, as if he was being drowned beneath frozen waters. Leonardo's heartbeat multiplied, and his breathing became heavier. A sudden shock came over his body, and voices of the lost souls of dark creatures began to fill the void in the empty room. Flashbacks of his family rose from deep within his thoughts. Leonardo began to remember the happiness he felt as a boy, when he shared joyful moments with his sister.

Never look down, my dear brother. Always look up and smile as if anything in life is possible. Never be afraid.

The words of his sister became loud and clear in his mind, like an echo rippling through the mountains. These were the words she had always made sure Leonardo would remember. His heart was mourning the loss of his family while the wave of shock was slowly and painfully killing him. No normal human being would have been able to handle such pain for as long as Leonardo did.

Suddenly, everything stopped. There was no more pain, no more voices, no more blood, and no more memories. Leonardo finally began to transform into what the mysterious man had intended him to become. Leonardo's eyes turned a golden hue that could shine in the darkest of nights. He grew a set of sharp canine teeth that went with his long, sharp nails. An uplifting power settled over Leonardo, making him feel stronger and more alive. This new inner power had finally overtaken his body and mind, making him feel like he had been born again.

This was all caused from the event that occurred last night with the strange man, Leonardo thought.

He had thought he was on the verge of dying, and now Leonardo felt a great pleasure in knowing he had been given a second chance at life. Anxious to start his new life, he went outside and stood behind the cabin underneath the night sky. He took a long, deep breath and thanked the heavens that he was still alive. As Leonardo was outside with his newly formed body, he noticed something white reflecting in the pond close by. He went to take a closer look but realized that *he* was the white reflection. Leonardo stood in shock of what he saw looking back at him. He had been transformed into what he thought existed in legends or myths to scare the children away from the woods. This was only a nightmare, he thought, as he splashed the reflection in the water. Nothing changed. Looking closely at his reflection, he saw his canine teeth, and with fear of what he had become, he moved away from what he saw. Leonardo took a good look at himself, touching his teeth and feeling the new features of his face. He ran his fingers through his hair that was now smooth and straight and to his shoulders, making him appear more attractive, elegant, and high class.

He could now see the horrifying truth that had become his new identity. Leonardo had become what people feared most. He had become a creature that lingered in the shadows, whose origins were unknown to many, and whose powers were deadly for humans. He had become a creature known to feed on blood, a creature that would live for all eternity. He had become a vampire.

IV

A cold breeze suddenly passed through Leonardo as he was walking back to his cabin. He opened the door, and fear ran down his spine. The man responsible for this nightmare appeared from the corner. He began to wonder why this man had decided to turn him into this creature. There were millions of people in the world, yet he chose him to be this nocturnal being.

"Feels good, doesn't it?" the man asked with a sinister smile. "You are now stronger and faster, and you never looked better, my friend."

"What did you do to me?" Leonardo asked, wondering about the change that was flowing through his veins.

"I gave you what you wanted. I gave you a life of fulfillment, a life without sickness, death, or pain. A life without the morals and principles that make up the foundation that humankind has dealt with since the beginning of time. Look at yourself. A newly born vampire has awakened from the hells of earth!"

He saw his reflection in the mirror that was hanging over the piano—a dead corpse. The mirror reflected a man with skin barely hanging on his bones and gray hair that was falling out. He jumped back, startled at what he saw.

"What did you see?" asked the man.

"I ... I saw myself as a corpse. I could not see who I was. How can this be?"

"What you saw reflecting back is unfortunately the truth behind our power and our beauty, but do not be troubled by it, Leonardo. We can only see our true selves through our reflection but not by humanity. We may be corpses inheriting the earth; we may even be called the undead, the cursed, and the damned that have fallen from grace. But remember, Leonardo, we are powerful, beautiful, and the fiercest creatures of the night for the rest of eternity."

Leonardo looked at him with fierce eyes. He realized that this man had killed him and then brought him back to be reborn again into this world.

"We will talk more about your changes later, but now you must be hungry."

"I am," Leonardo said as the thirst for blood pierced his throat.

"Come, I will show you the ways of being a vampire. However, before I do, you must vow to me that you will learn everything you need to know. You must also vow to never reveal who we are to any human, no matter how significant they are to you."

Leonardo shook the man's hand in agreement to his conditions. He knew that in order for him to understand what he had become, and to become a true vampire, he had to learn first from his maker.

"I want to know everything."

"Follow me," the man said, heading out of the cabin as Leonardo followed behind.

*　　*　　*　　*

In the meantime, Mr. Cooper was enjoying his favorite glass of scotch. Suddenly, he heard a knock at the door.

"Who the hell is knocking on my door at this time of night?" Mr. Cooper said as he got up and headed toward the door. "Who's there?"

There was no answer. He asked again, but again there was no answer. Frustrated, Mr. Cooper headed back to his study to continue his drink, but again, he heard another knock. He stomped his way back to the door and this time opened the door to confront whoever was disturbing him.

"Leonardo!" he said sternly, confused at the sight of him. "For God's sake! What is this? Leonardo, what in the devil's name is going on here! I thought you were dying—no, you were dead! You tricked me. How dare you come …"

Mr. Cooper felt a sense of fear run through him. Something was not right.

"Who on earth is that man standing behind you? Why is he on my land?" He yelled while gesturing towards the strange man.

While Leonardo was trying to figure out a way to explain everything to Mr. Cooper, he felt a strong urge inside that was craving the taste of blood. This urge was tempting him to attack Mr. Cooper and feed on his blood.

His maker, standing behind him, reached out and put his hand on Leonardo's shoulder, silently demanding him to feed. Leonardo fought the urge for a brief moment, overpowering his new instincts that almost made him attack Mr. Cooper like a wild animal without self-control. Mr. Cooper may have treated him badly and punished him often, but he gave him a roof over his head and clothes on his back. Nevertheless, the man did not care about the feelings Leonardo had towards Mr. Cooper. As Mr. Cooper's hand rose up to slap Leonardo in the face for not responding to his question, Leonardo's instincts kicked in, and this time he charged at him without restraint.

Mr. Cooper was thrown across the room; he yelled and tried to push Leonardo away from him. The next thing he knew, Leonardo had pulled him off the ground. A strength that neither both fully understood. Leonardo couldn't resist how incredible yet, terrifying this new power was rising from within him. He then slammed him against the floor. Pinning Mr. Cooper to the floor, Leonardo saw a vein appear on the side of his neck. His insides burning with the thirst for blood, he sank his teeth into Mr. Cooper's neck and began to drink his blood. Mr. Cooper tried to push him away, but there was no use; he could not match Leonardo's strength, now that his blood was being drained from his body. Witnessing Mr. Cooper's death, Leonardo's maker laughed and rejoiced in pride.

Having the peace and satisfaction of his first victim, Leonardo continued to drink Mr. Cooper's blood, trying to calm his thirst. His maker came up behind him and pulled him away, gently but with enough force to make him stop.

"Stop, Leonardo. You should never fully drain the body of blood. If you do, death will control you and make your victim's soul haunt you forever."

He looked at his maker in fear, yet with blood covering his lips, he was gratified. Pulling himself up off of Mr. Cooper's body, Leonardo felt a power that rewarded all of his anger toward Mr. Cooper. The man took hold of Mr. Cooper's head and swiftly made a sharp twist that ended his life.

"How do you feel, Leonardo?" He asked with a cunning smile.

"I feel ... satisfied," Leonardo replied with a relief.

"Good. Now let's get rid of the body and go to a more secure place."

After miles of walking from Mr. Cooper's land and taking the time to burn his body, the man took Leonardo to a land near the Allegheny River that was filled with rows of tombstones. Leonardo was astonished to see how full the land was; it seemed to be the land of forgotten souls. The man demanded that Leonardo stay with him among the land of the dead for the night. Having no other option, Leonardo obeyed his command. After they walked through the unkempt and overgrown grass that protected each grave, they entered a small and crumbling mausoleum. The man led the way through the dark and empty chamber, taking Leonardo to the end of the room where six stone tombs lay closed against the chamber walls. Various floor-length candelabras dimly illuminated the cobwebs that hung among the corners and cracks of the decomposing bodies and the lifeless mausoleum. Everything inside was left carelessly untouched to leave the forgotten souls at peace. Leonardo followed the man to one of the six coffins that occupied the chamber and watched as the man lifted the top of the coffin, releasing the suffocating air of the dead corpse that lay inside. He tossed the remains of the restful body onto the pile of the other decomposing bodies on the floor.

"This here, my friend, is where you will rest. From the moment the sunrises to when the sunsets, you will sleep within this coffin," the man said, introducing the most basic custom known to vampires.

Leonardo became uneasy, given the thought that he would be confined to a closed space all through the day, in addition to the fact that the coffin had belonged to someone else. Again, he obeyed his maker without protest.

"Once the day has turned into dark, I shall teach you how to embrace your dark gift as an immortal. Tomorrow night, you will find your next feast to be rather interesting."

As Leonardo began to climb inside the tomb to start his new life as a vampire, he still had a question that needed to be answered.

"Who are you?" Leonardo asked with curiosity.

"My name is Boris. Boris De La' Vega," he answered with a smile as he closed his coffin, ending the final day of a new beginning.

V

The sun had risen for a new day, and the mortals went about their lives. Some went on to experience new possibilities, while for others; their lives stayed the same. The world had grown another day older, and after a long day of work, the night had fallen upon the sky once again.

Making their way out from the mausoleum to a path that lay ahead of them, Boris knew where he needed to take Leonardo. However, before they would reach their destination, Boris wanted to test Leonardo's primitive instincts. From a distance, Boris caught sight of a priest leaving the town's church that owned the cemetery; suddenly he knew that the best way to break Leonardo in was to pressure him to take the life of somebody that the mortals believed represented light and holiness. This was how to teach Leonardo the ways of being a vampire.

The priest was a slender man, with the promise of love and hope emanating from him. Making sure that everything was in place outside of the church for the next day, he was unaware of anything going on in the cemetery that rested some distance away from him. As they moved among the shadows, careful not to scare away their prey, Boris grabbed Leonardo by the arm, stopping them in their tracks.

"What are we doing here?" Leonardo asked.

"Listen here. These are the ways we live and survive, and you need to accept that. This is what we do. It is in our nature. Now, come with me."

Without a second thought, Boris told Leonardo to follow him to the church. As the distance between them and the priest shortened, Boris could sense that Leonardo was becoming uncertain about the situation, especially what he was about to ask him to do. He never once thought that he would be asked to ever harm a man of faith. Nevertheless, Leonardo understood that he had to obey his master, so he agreed to what had to be done.

They gracefully approached the priest, expressing their seductive presence while the man was startled at their sudden appearance from the cemetery.

"How can I service you, gentlemen?" the priest asked in fear, but also curious about who they were.

To Leonardo's surprise, it was as if Boris had become a completely different person when he replied to the priest. "I am only a man who is seeking the word of your holiness, and my friend here is also very fond of the hope you bring to the townspeople."

"The words I share are from scriptures that have been passed down through generations from our brothers and sisters," the priest explained as he fell under the vampire's hypnosis.

Boris called for Leonardo to come and introduce himself to the priest and led him away from the church back toward the gloomy abyss of the cemetery. It was quiet, except for the faint chirping of crows and the trees brushing up against the wind. Meanwhile, the priest was oblivious of the danger he was in, and his curiosity was taken over by Leonardo's and Boris's charm and beauty. As Boris kept a watchful distance from behind them, the priest followed Leonardo, asking what they wanted to know about the scriptures.

Without bothering to answer the priest, Boris leaped from behind and wrapped his arm around his neck. Boris used his strength to hold the struggling priest in place.

"What are you doing? Please, sir, I have done nothing!" the priest exclaimed, struggling to get away from under Boris' grasp.

"You are purely living; that is what you have," Boris responded, finally coming out of his character, unbothered by the struggle of the man. It seemed so easy for Boris to turn into a monstrous creature. "Leonardo, now it is your chance to take his life."

"No!" the priest pleaded. "Please have mercy on my soul."

In spite of how evil this act seemed to Leonardo, he could not deny feeling the yearning sensation for blood that would quench his hunger. As if his body took over, the next thing Leonardo felt was his fangs tearing into the flesh of the faithful priest. Blood splattered across the watchful eyes of an overbearing angel that protected a nearby grave, and the priest's warm, pure blood coursed through Leonardo. It was as if he had never tasted anything more pleasurable in his entire life. Boris held the priest and stood by, overpowering Leonardo to push him toward his growing need. Leonardo felt more and more overwhelmed.

The priest began to feel faint but felt little pain, knowing that his life was out of his control now. As Leonardo aggressively drank his blood, sudden flashes invaded his mind; he could hear agonizing screams of a young boy as he witnessed the horrifying flashbacks of the priest being beaten and bruised to near death by his father. This was a man who grew up being tortured by his own family. A similar pain to which reminded Leonardo about his childhood with his father. It wasn't the way he had imagined the priest's life to have been. With this realization, he quickly opened his eyes and pulled away.

"I can't do this . . . I will not kill him," he said, feeling guilty. He took the priest from his grasp and laid him on the ground, weakened.

Boris was furious at Leonardo for not finishing what he started but then realized what had happened to make Leonardo stop. Leonardo started to move away from the scene with great shame because he was taking the life of an innocent man, one who represented the symbols of sacredness and compassion. Taking the priest's mortal life was too much for Leonardo to bear. Flashes of his family's death went through his mind, and he remembered how it all once was and how happy his life seemed to be then.

"It's beautiful, isn't it, Leonardo. The first taste of blood for the night is always so exhilarating," Boris said. "It is because of that you couldn't control your instincts to take the life of this man, yet it seemed that his past troubled you. Probably why you couldn't finish it. What a shame."

Boris grabbed the nearly dead priest's body off the ground and drank the last few ounces of his blood, ending his life. Then suddenly, before Leonardo could stop him, Boris cracked his neck. Without dignity or peace for the dead, Boris dragged his body by the feet across the cemetery grounds and threw him into an empty six-foot grave, as if the priest was nothing but worthless trash. They both stood by the edge of the grave, staring down and witnessing the end of the humble and innocent priest lying inside the grave before them. Seeing the dead body of the priest lying in the dirt, all Leonardo could remember was how the priest was mistreated as a young boy by his father, and then he realized that he was no better than the priest's father. To Boris, this was about nothing more than just satisfying a thirst, yet to Leonardo, the man had failed to free the guilt of his true inner self.

Boris could sense what Leonardo was going through and reminded him of when he himself traveled through the dark times in England, searching, stealing, and killing in order to learn how to live on his own as a vampire, after his maker had abandoned him to face immortality alone four hundred years ago.

"Living in the shadows fills one with guilt and regret, which only bring upon suffering," Boris said. "Learning the truth of our survival was one of the most difficult consequences I had to endure for a long time, but it was necessary. Trying to live your immortal life with mortal coil would only bring despair and unwanted misery. One must do what our nature intended us to do."

"So, I see."

"Now, what did you learn from this, Leonardo?" Boris asked.

"That I shouldn't take a human life without a purpose," Leonardo replied.

Boris laughed at Leonardo's answer. He knew there was much Leonardo had to learn in order for him to gain the knowledge and understanding of what the true essence of being an immortal vampire really was.

"No. Tonight was for you to learn how to survive. The purpose is for you to feed. You cannot give into their past or present sufferings. If you do, you will never be able to find peace. Would you rather feel their pain instead of being able to free yours? My friend, you need to learn how to embrace this new life, because from here on out, it is all in your hands."

"Does it have to be like this? To kill and treat mortals as if they are worthless in order for us to feed our cravings and to survive? It's madness!" Leonardo yelled, now facing him.

"You will soon understand, Leonardo. It's just a matter of time and patience until you give in, and then you won't be able to turn back."

"I can try to resist it," Leonardo said with some hope of finding another way to live.

"Many have tried, and many have failed," Boris said as he turned his back to Leonardo.

With disappointment, Leonardo and Boris both headed back inside the mausoleum for another night in hiding. Boris knew that Leonardo wasn't ready but was hopeful that he would learn from what he planned for the coming night.

VI

The hooded figure came unwelcomed into the house of a farmer and his family. The figure was on a mission to kill a destined immortal that would grow to destroy what they had been in a period of centuries. Heading up the stairs, threats and screams were suddenly being thrown at him. There wasn't time for this; the first to be killed was a young boy, who was trying to escape in one of the rooms. His blood was young and warm as the hooded figure ripped into the flesh that was his neck. After tossing the young boy aside, the figure took the lives of the farmer and his wife, and as he turned to continue on with the next victim, he caught sight of himself in the mirror. Horrified at what the figure saw looking back at him, he screamed in agony, as the reflection was Leonardo in skin and bones.

Leonardo woke up, startled from the nightmare. Pushing aside the lid of the tomb, he saw Boris standing against the wall of the entrance, staring out toward the moonlight.

"It's about time you woke up. You were mumbling in your sleep again, which could have gotten us killed if they found us," Boris complained, still staring out at the night sky.

Not knowing how to respond, as Leonardo was surprised that he had been talking in his sleep, he got out of the tomb in hopes that this night would be better than the last.

"Before we continue on our passage, there is another place I would like to take you," Boris said, turning toward a lone rat that crept against the edge of the wall. With a sudden movement, the rat lay lifeless and drained. "Get yourself ready, for we need to be there shortly," Boris continued to say, as he gracefully wiped blood from his lips.

Boris decided to test Leonardo again by taking him to the most talked about banquet of the year. Sir Jonathan Williams, a wealthy politician, was hosting the banquet in celebration of the engagement of his only daughter, the twenty-year-old Elizabeth Williams. It was at these kinds of events that Boris prided himself in his skills of hunting his prey and finding fresh blood to feed on.

The celebrated events were all the same; gorgeous women were married to rich and unfaithful husbands, and they would hide their loneliness behind their vanity and their lavish, embroidered gowns. Though Boris had a desire for lonely women, he was also fond of preying on young men, most of who were blinded by wealth and power. Usually, it was the young who Boris was drawn to feed on. Moreover, they were drawn to him, both sexually and emotionally. All vampires were cursed with the dark gift of seduction.

Together, they entered the exquisite mansion of the Williams, and all eyes were on them as they walked through the doors. Leonardo couldn't take his eyes off of all the elegance that immersed the mansion, and the rich townspeople that occupied it. Boris walked in with elegance, pride, and confidence; it seemed he was the ruler of the land. Whispers and laughter echoed throughout the room; the townspeople had suspicions of what they were, but they never dared stand against Boris or anyone that accompanied him. They knew that if they did, Boris would strike fear within their mortal souls, and they would wish they were dead rather than alive. In the event that Boris attended, he was always seen as a mysterious aristocrat that had always managed to seduce the most beautiful women in his presence. No one has been able to resist his unquestionable charms, that would captivate their imagination.

As for Leonardo, he was still trying to get comfortable with the stares of the mortals that followed his every movement. Walking through the crowd of people that came to celebrate a long-awaited marriage, no one mattered to Boris, not even the desperate, lonely women or the drunken people that just came for the alcohol. He was there to find the one mortal that would satisfy his needs for the start of the night. Boris began looking for the next victim for Leonardo and himself by reading their thoughts and understanding their feelings. Meanwhile, Leonardo was becoming overwhelmed by his hunger and thirst for blood. It was gradually becoming more and more unbearable for him. As Leonardo and Boris passed through the crowd of people inside the banquet, Leonardo realized that the people who attended were those who had treated him like worthless trash when he was a mortal. Now he saw them as food to quench his thirst, like a buffet for his choosing. It was the unbearable truth; he would have to accept the hunger one way or another. To many who attended that banquet, fine wine and liquor had filled the air. However, Leonardo realized that he found himself not caring for such things. He desired only one craving, which was of human blood.

As small talk began between people, Leonardo became distracted by an abundant scent from a distance. He followed the scent, and it led him to a gorgeous young girl flirting in a crowd of young soldiers. Suddenly he remembered Elizabeth had once come into Mr. Cooper's house with her cousin Sir Michael Hewitt to discuss the crop business. That same day, he laid his eyes on her gentle and kind heart, and it seized his soul for a brief moment. In Leonardo's eyes, she was the only person in the room. She had beautiful red hair that brought out her blue eyes and her soft, pale skin.

"It seems that beautiful young woman has her eye on you, Leonardo," Boris observed.

"What about her?" he asked, catching another glimpse of the woman.

"Her name is Elizabeth Williams, the only daughter of one of the town politicians and the future wife of Derek Hughes," Boris whispered in his ear.

Derek had walked over to her and asked her for a dance. They began to dance together with grace and pride for everyone to see. Leonardo could not help but stare at her elegance and beauty. Boris, standing close by, noticed that Leonardo wanted her. Reading Boris's mind, Leonardo began to use his gift and with his vampire eyes began to seduce her to come to him.

As Elizabeth was dancing, she began to feel that someone was watching her. She turned and moved with the rhythm of the music, but she was more focused on finding the pair of eyes that were watching her so attentively. She noticed that it was Leonardo who was across the room looking at her with desire lingering in his eyes. Every time Derek turned her around, she tried to make eye contact with him, and every time they did, an indescribable attraction started to develop between them.

"She wants you as much as you want her, Leonardo," Boris whispered from behind him.

Leonardo did not want to be tempted to drink her blood; he wanted to prevent the incident that happened the night before with the priest. However, Boris was not amused by Leonardo's feelings towards the humans. Using his telepathic powers, he took control and pushed Leonardo to feed on her.

Something inside Leonardo took over, tempting him to crave her blood. When the song was over, Elizabeth left Derek's side and seductively went up to Leonardo and Boris, who were standing across the room.

"Hello, gentlemen. I hope that you are both enjoying yourselves tonight," Elizabeth said, with desire in her voice.

"Yes, we are, dear Elizabeth. Perhaps you could help us with something. My friend here would like to see if you have a few moments to spare to accompany him for a dance," Boris replied.

"Is that right, sir?" Elizabeth asked, smiling seductively at Leonardo.

"Most certainly," Boris replied.

He left them alone, confident that Leonardo would not back out again. Elizabeth was falling under Leonardo's seduction. She stood by him, sliding her hand against his arm, unaware of what others around them might see. While Leonardo could feel every blood cell flow through her body, he let go of his emotions and surrendered to his vampire lust.

"May I have this dance?" Leonardo asked as he put his hand out for hers.

"Of course," Elizabeth replied, putting her hand on his.

Boris was relieved and impressed that Leonardo was finally letting go and starting to trust his instincts. However, he could feel a strong sense of jealously coming from Elizabeth's fiancé, Derek, who was watching his future wife dance passionately with another man. While Boris was keeping a watchful eye out for Derek, he was pleased to see Leonardo's true nature beginning to flourish.

On the dance floor, Leonardo was gracefully twirling Elizabeth around, extending her out and bringing her back into his arms as their eyes locked together. He wanted to see the soul that he would be taking tonight. Elizabeth was serenaded by his charm and mesmerized by the look in his eyes. Mastering the skill of seduction against a mortal human was a difficult task for a newborn vampire; however, for Leonardo, it seemed to come naturally. The more they danced the more Elizabeth felt that she had seen him somewhere before but couldn't remember completely. Glimpses of the slave she became fond of in Mr. Cooper's land came into mind. Remembering those gentle eyes, and his humble face, it couldn't possibly be him, she thought. That man seemed so different than the man she was dancing with, both having similar features yet so unbearably different.

"You look familiar. Have we met before?" Elizabeth asked, gazing deeply within his eyes.

"Not properly I'm afraid," Leonardo replied as he looked into her eyes. "How did you learn how to dance so gracefully?" she asked breathlessly. "I just do," Leonardo answered with a slight grin.

Elizabeth moved closer to him, pressing herself against his body as she put her lips near his ear and whispered pleasurable things to him. Her hand began to caress his cold, pale body, and Leonardo could not avoid it; all he could do was let go of his guilt and his past and give into what he had become. Elizabeth followed his seductive movements, with the attraction getting stronger and stronger. It was as if fire was running through the core of her body, making her feel as if Leonardo was the only person that mattered in the world. Leonardo touched her body and was moved by her softness. His vampire essence erupted inside of him, overtaking the last human thought and leaving a cold, immortal body. The only thought he had at that moment was the feel of her gorgeous skin, her gleaming blue eyes, her red hair, and her natural, full lips. None of that mattered though for Leonardo, as all he desired was to drink her blood. Leonardo led Elizabeth across the dance floor, as he knew it would be her last night. He could hear nothing but her steady breathing and her escalating heartbeat. Leonardo took Elizabeth's hands and gently kissed them with his cold lips, and pleasure spread throughout her body; he had learned now how easy it was to seduce a woman. Leonardo could feel his power over her—the taking of a mortal life and turning it into blood to feed on, making her yearn for him as she reached her deepest desires, and feeling the acceptance of the dark supremacy that surrounded them.

Boris, satisfied with the progress that Leonardo was making, was keeping an eye out for Derek, who was furious at what was going on between Elizabeth and Leonardo. Boris knew that if anyone tried to interfere while they preyed on their victim, they would be killed in an instant. It was known in the vampire world that when a mortal interrupted a vampire, their face would never be forgotten until the opportune moment came when they were hunted down, and death would follow as their punishment.

Leonardo continued to dance with Elizabeth, and she was becoming his puppet. She could not help the adrenaline running through her body, which gave her the desire to kiss him as he kissed her back. Leonardo moved his lips away and made his way to her neck, desperately wanting to bite down. Elizabeth, perplexed by the man standing before her, grabbed Leonardo's cold arms and pulled him closer. She wanted him, and as hard it was for

Leonardo to avoid the lust he had for her, he wanted her too. "Make me yours," Elizabeth whispered to him. Leonardo began to open his mouth and was getting ready to bite into her neck, but suddenly flashes emerged of his mother's dead body covered in blood. As he pulled away from her neck, Derek approached them and grabbed Elizabeth's arm, furiously pulling her away from Leonardo.

"Get your hands off of her!" He said.

"Please Derek, no!" Elizabeth yelled. With Derek's fist in the air about to hit Leonardo's face, Boris immediately appeared in the middle of the scene, giving a low, menacing growl.

With his fierce eyes, he said, "I wouldn't dare go that far if I were you. It will be the biggest regret of your life. It will only cause you pain, and there will be no mercy." Elizabeth was beginning to feel frightened from the dark look Boris was expressing.

"Please, Derek, don't harm them. Let them be," Elizabeth said as she stood by Derek's side.

"Quiet! Don't be more of an embarrassment to me, Elizabeth," Derek yelled, pulling away from her. "I suggest that both you gentlemen leave now, or I will call the authorities!"

Everyone's eyes were on them. Boris felt disgraced by Leonardo's incompetent desire to bite Elizabeth before Derek interrupted them. Sir Williams came up to them to find out what the commotion was all about and to try to settle it before it got out of hand.

"Sir Williams, I am sorry for the disturbance. I and many others here have witnessed this man here seducing Elizabeth! Derek explained.

"Elizabeth, is this true?" Sir Williams asked.

"Unfortunately, it's true. I saw everything from the distance. Even for a second, I thought I had lost the love of my life to this bastard. This man, and his companion have caused nothing but trouble on our important occasion," Derek answered for her.

"Father, it's not what it seemed, I promise." Elizabeth said trying to hold back her tears.

"Enough, Elizabeth! There is no more to be said about your bold behavior tonight."

After a thoughtful moment, Sir Williams was convinced that Boris and Leonardo had started the conflict. He firmly asked them to leave and said that they were never to come back on his land. He even suggested that they leave town so that the respectful citizens of Pittsburgh could live in peace. Boris was disappointed in Leonardo and what he had caused tonight, and in that moment, he regretted making Leonardo a vampire.

"If that is how you feel, we will obey, sir," Boris said, as he knew that it would not be proper to slaughter them all in that moment.

Boris then turned to Derek and said, "Soon you will learn the consequences of what happens when someone tries to get between my affairs."

Then Boris turned and walked away from the scene, with Leonardo following behind him.

Distancing themselves from the mansion, they reached deep into the pine trees when Boris pulled Leonardo aside to confront him about what happened back at the banquet.

"Haven't you learned anything, Leonardo? You need to control these foolish thoughts of yours! Why do you do this to me?"

"Because I would rather die and burn from the flames of hell than become a killer like you!" Leonardo yelled in anger towards Boris. "Even if it means sacrificing any human thoughts I have left. You gave me no choice in accepting this horrendous life!"

"Then I should have left you in the woods to rot and die! That way, I wouldn't have to see you turning into the pitiful and pathetic vampire that you have become!"

"I never wanted to become this—an immortal living in a world that is forever changing. If this is who I was meant to be through God's eyes, then so be it. I will choose my own way!" Leonardo said, as his words made Boris more upset.

"You think an arrogant newborn vampire like yourself who feels pity for the humans and is haunted by a past life can find his own way? You think you can just walk around in this world and ignore the rules that have been passed down for centuries? You, my dear friend, have fallen from grace. That you cannot change. You are a sinner, a killer like me and the rest of the world, Leonardo!"

Leonardo's anger had boiled over. He knew that something had to be done to the one who gave him this curse. Leonardo charged at him with as much force as his body could give, in hopes of grabbing Boris's neck and slamming his head against the tree. Nevertheless, Boris, being over four hundred years old, knew what to expect. He quickly got a hold of Leonardo's neck in a flash of light and instead slammed Leonardo into the tree. With all the power and strength Boris gave, it took a toll on the tree, and it fell to the ground. Leonardo knew he had no chance to fight and win against Boris, not until he was able to control his emotions and understand the ways of being a vampire. There was no point in fighting because he could not overpower Boris. He gave in, and Boris freed him from his grasp.

"Next time you dare to defy me, I promise you that I will rip your cold heart out of your corpse, and you will not see another night again! Is that understood?" Boris said as he tried to control his temper.

Leonardo nodded in agreement as he looked away from Boris, not wanting to look directly in his eyes.

"Don't be afraid, Leonardo," Boris said, leaning towards him. "After all, we are nothing if not creatures of the dark." He turned and suddenly disappeared in a flash of light.

Leonardo stayed behind to contemplate what had just happened. He felt sorry for disappointing Boris again, but he believed that there was no way to get rid of his past, no matter how hard he tried. Feeling ashamed that he could not become what Boris wanted him to be, a powerful, bloodthirsty, strong vampire, he felt broken and full of despair. He was overwhelmed with anger and felt worthless. It seemed as if the world had turned on him when suddenly he heard someone a few yards away heading towards him. The thirst for blood was suffocating every drop of air from his lungs and took control. He went straight for the man, a curious politician that had followed them from the banquet. His vampire instincts took control, and within seconds, he found the man standing in shock at his sudden appearance. He grabbed the man by the collar, turned his neck to the side, and aggressively dug his teeth through his skin. The blood felt so warm and satisfying to Leonardo; he could feel the blood caress every dead organ and hollow bone in his body. The man was dead in seconds, and minutes later, his blood fulfilled Leonardo. Pulling back and letting go of the man, Leonardo realized what he just did. Satisfaction turned into guilt, as he had made his first kill as a vampire. He killed knowing that he had an innocent man's blood on his hands. His thirst took the better of him, and he knew that Boris could never know about this. Giving the dead man some shred of dignity, Leonardo cleaned the blood off the man's body and dug a grave with his bare hands to give him a proper burial. With his fast vampire gifts, he quickly dug six feet into the ground and gently placed the man inside. Before putting the dirt back in, Leonardo closed his eyes and offered a moment of silence in honor of the man. Everything seemed to be going wrong, no matter what he chose to do.

Half an hour later, Leonardo completed the burial; however, he knew what he had to do for forgiveness. He walked a few miles away from the grave and sat underneath a pine tree, waiting to see the sunrise again. Leonardo thought of nothing; he just sat there looking up into the sky, waiting to feel the warmth of the sun on his body once more. The stillness of the world made three hours seem like three minutes, until the sunrise appeared.

Abruptly, Leonardo felt a dark essence appear.

"What are you trying to do, Leonardo?" Boris asked, appearing from behind the tree.

From the look on Boris's face, Leonardo knew that he was upset, but that did not matter to him anymore.

"I want to see the sunrise."

"Are you mad? Do you have any idea what you are doing?" asked Boris. "It will burn you and turn you into ash. It will be a slow and agonizing way to your death. And I will not let you do that to yourself!"

"Why would you even care if I die or not? Haven't I disappointed you enough? The real question is, why me? Why did you choose to give me this life, Boris?"

"I felt pity for you, Leonardo. I believed that you could have been a powerful vampire." Boris knelt down in front of him. "I saw myself in you. I chose to have hope in you."

"I'd rather you killed me than made me into this!" Leonardo replied.

"Leonardo, understand this: when I turned, I became an angry and selfish vampire. Tabitha the beautiful was her name; she gave me this life, and even though the moments we shared together were breathtaking, my life had no purpose, no order, and I was not able to accept my new reality. The reality was that we are all alone in the end, and I did not ask for nor did I desire a mortal or an immortal life. But since I came to terms with it, I have enjoyed every moment of being a vampire, without any regrets ... until now."

Boris's expression turned from satisfaction and happiness to a suffering pain that came from deep within his past. He wondered what happened to Tabitha.

"Come with me," Boris said while stretching his hand to Leonardo. "You are my prodigy, my brother, my friend. Please, Leonardo."

Leonardo thought about the pain Boris went through, and he came to the realization that they had much more in common. After listening to what Boris had to say, he decided to be more open about his decisions so that Boris could lead him to become a true vampire.

As soon as Leonardo got up, Boris heard rapid footsteps coming from the distance. Immediately he realized that the town's authorities sent by Sir Williams were on their way to arrest them both. In this town, rumors spread like wildflowers. Boris took Leonardo by the arm and sped away into the dark woods, protecting them from the flying bullets and lanterns. The authorities who witnessed this amazing ability from the distance were shocked and frightened, never in their lives had they seen men run with incredible speed. Boris knew Leonardo was not fully ready to handle such conflict, even though he could have killed all seven officers if he wanted to. He chose not to take that chance.

Leonardo was astonished to feel his full ability thrive as he ran at such a brilliant speed that it seemed that he was flying. He could feel the air breezing through his hair and clothes, and it was an indescribable feeling. The trees and wilderness around them seemed to rapidly pass by, making it seem impossible for any other being to achieve such powers. But there was one condition to having those kinds of abilities; the darker and older a vampire became, the more their gifts grew stronger and more natural to them, and once their gifts were mastered, new abilities would gradually develop.

They arrived in a cave just a few miles from the Williams' banquet. Inside this cave was an unusual scent and dark feeling. It seemed that the cave had a mysterious omen within it, as if they were not the only immortals that had stayed in it. As they walked through the open mouth of the cave, Boris appeared to be unbothered by the omen that erupted from inside; it seemed that he had visited the cave many times before. The cave definitely was no resting place for any mortal since it was filled with gloom and night insects. "Why are we here, Boris?" Leonardo asked. Boris, irritated and frustrated, explained that the authorities of the town had been looking for the murderers of the priest and Matthew Cooper. With the events that unfolded at the banquet, it was enough to suspect them as murderers. Leonardo then asked him what the best thing to do was. Boris looked at him as if Leonardo had asked a foolish question.

"The last thing we need is to draw any further attention to us. We are meant to stay out of the human world. We cannot be seen or heard or even socialize with any mortal because that would present the risk of uncovering what we are. We appear to them only when we hunt and kill them."

"So, why did you take me to the banquet?" Leonardo asked. "Who made these ridiculous rules of whether vampires can or cannot socialize with mortals? And who says we have to follow them?"

"It doesn't matter who created our way of living; we have lived this way for so long, Leonardo. For centuries, no vampire has ever dared to betray our race."

Leonardo was confused.

"You thought it was just you and I?" Boris asked with a soft laugh. "We are immortals. We live forever, my friend, and we are not the only ones."

Leonardo was shocked to hear that they had the power to live for all eternity. A mediocre question that he had overlooked since the beginning. How could he have not known this fact since the moment he had turn? They could live with no sickness, no fatal accidents, and no aging. It all sounded amazing, but the mere thought of having to endure this evil for life's eternity was torture.

Dawn was approaching, and Boris headed to the walls of the cave and started to climb up. Leonardo was amazed; he looked like a spider climbing the wall. Boris got all the way to the top, standing above Leonardo. He let go of his hands against the wall and just hung from his feet, upside down like a real bat. He crossed his arms and began to sleep as if it were normal. Surprised and amazed at witnessing yet another incredible ability of a vampire, Leonardo became doubtful of his powers and newborn abilities. He managed to climb the cave wall but not without falling. Leonardo figured there was no possible way to learn this ability overnight. He decided to sleep on the ground away from the rays of sunlight peeking through parts of the cave, while Boris slept fifty feet above him, waiting for the next night.

* * * *

Back at the town, citizens began to run back into their houses, and the homeless began to seek shelter in fear while armed officers continued their search for Boris and Leonardo. They were hoping that they would find and sentence them to be hanged for the murder of the priest and Matthew Cooper. Search parties were dispatch to find them in the woods, but their mission was unsuccessful. To them it had seemed as if Boris and Leonardo had vanished out of thin air without a trace of evidence.

VII

As the sunset covered the day and night fell upon them, Leonardo woke up to a conversation inside the cave. When he got up to see who it was, he saw Boris talking to someone he did not recognize. He later found out from Boris that the man was a five hundred-year-old vampire from England and went by the name of Lucius Thorne. Lucius was six feet tall with a slim figure and unlike any other vampire. Lucius was known for his unique vampire gifts: levitation and telekinesis. He had long blond hair that was combed back and deep blue eyes that could deceive any mortal, seducing them with a single glance. Lucius appeared to be wearing a very sophisticated black waistcoat over a white linen blouse and black breeches, all underneath a dark gray coat. He came from a high-class background, which helped him to become a very clever vampire who had over the years learned how to manipulate mortals and live comfortably in the mortal world.

As Leonardo curiously approached them, he had a suspicious feeling that Lucius was not to be trusted.

"Ah! You must be Leonardo. Am I right?" Lucius asked. "Boris has told me so much about you."

"I suppose he has told you about all the problems I have caused," Leonardo replied.

"Unfortunately, he has," Lucius answered.

"Well, if you are one of us, then how come Boris has never mentioned you before?" Leonardo asked.

"You know, even though we barely just met, I can already see that you have much to learn. You have barely begun your new journey as a newborn," said Lucius, narrowing his eyes.

Without losing eye contact with Lucius, Leonardo asked Boris what the progress was on the officers that were looking for them, and if they were safe enough in the cave during the day. Boris explained that the townspeople believed that a witch cursed the cave many years ago, and anyone who had a cruel heart that was filled with vanity or hatred would suffer horrible consequences until death came and found them. Lucius interrupted to explain that there was no need to worry; witch curses and spells could not harm elder vampires. Their spells only affected those who were weak minded, like mortals, and in some cases newborn vampires.

"Witches?" Leonardo asked. "The tales and stories I heard as a child are true after all."

"Witches and warlocks, they can't harm us with their powers. As a matter of fact, they think we're their guide to true immortality. Such foolish creatures." Lucius said, shaking his head. "They are still our prey, yet they are too ignorant to see it."

"It is time for you to meet the rest of us, Leonardo," Boris chimed in with a sinister smile.

"Where are we going?" Leonardo asked, looking at Boris with raised eyebrows.

"To Romulus's castle," Lucius replied.

"Romulus?" Leonardo asked curiously.

"One of the oldest vampires living in this world today. Creator of our way of living and leader of the seven most powerful vampire covenants," Boris answered.

Leonardo couldn't help but feel curious to meet other vampires, especially Romulus. Waiting until Lucius walked away and was within some distance from them; Leonardo grabbed Boris by the sleeve, pulling him away to talk to him privately.

"What about us? Are we going to come back here?" Leonardo asked.

"No, we are not. We can't return because the entire town will be looking for us. There is nothing for us here anymore," Boris replied.

As Lucius approached Leonardo, he knew that Leonardo did not want to leave Pittsburgh. Lucius explained, glancing at his own sharp nails,"The best thing for you two to do is to either stay hidden, or move to another place far away from Pennsylvania, especially when you have a persistent newborn who attracts too much attention."

Leonardo, feeling as if his life had turned into a game, felt the same demands and disrespect he had when he was a mortal. Leonardo's anger erupted; he went up to Lucius and grabbed him by his blouse.

"Leonardo, don't!" Boris yelled.

Lucius reacted quickly, moving away as Boris managed to hold Leonardo back. Boris tried to calm Leonardo down, who yelled in anger, "I am tired of obeying orders and following rules! This is exactly what I've dealt with all through my life!" Lucius showed restraint, and controlled his fighting instincts, even though he knew that, with a single movement, he could have killed Leonardo faster than any mortal's eyes could see. He simply walked toward Leonardo, adjusting his clothes and pushing his hair back.

"Sometimes in order to survive, you must do what is necessary, Leonardo. Remember, the only thing that can get in our way is ourselves," Lucius said.

In the end, Leonardo felt there was no option other than to trust Boris and Lucius, so he agreed to go with them to Romulus's castle. Boris felt relieved that Leonardo had finally made a wise decision.

Lucius's carriage had just arrived to begin their journey to the far east of Pittsburgh. After Lucius opened the door, Leonardo went inside the carriage first. Before Boris stepped into the carriage, Lucius turned to him and said, "You need to keep your eyes on him."

With everyone in and settled down in the carriage for the long journey to Romulus's castle, dark clouds came upon the land in preparation of a great storm that was slowly approaching.

Hours passed, and Lucius maintained the carriage with ease. There was no sign of worry upon his flawless face; he and the carriage coach knew the way of the wilderness more than anyone else did. It was a land filled with dangerous hills and cliffs, where many had died trying to pass through.

"Why do we have to travel in a carriage? Why can't we just fly or run to our destination?" Leonardo asked.

"We prefer to travel in style most of the time. We can be civilized as well and not seem like the monsters that we are, or the monsters that are lurking about within the darkness," Lucius replied.

"There are other monsters?"

"Oh yes, there are other things lurking in the shadows besides us. Trust me—a newborn like yourself wouldn't want to be caught in their path," Lucius said, staring out into the wilderness. Sounds and howls of fierce werewolves could be heard from many miles away.

"Wolves?" Leonardo asked.

"Those are not ordinary wolves Leonardo," Boris replied as he exchanged smiles with Lucius.

"And that's just the beginning," Lucius said.

After some time, they finally arrived at their destination. Leonardo was amazed as he looked up and realized how enormous the castle was. It seemed to Leonardo that life within the castle had a long, unknown history; by stepping into the castle, he was going to learn a lot more secrets.

So, this is the castle of Romulus, Leonardo thought.

The mansion seemed to reach fifty feet into the sky and was built on the edge of a cliff by the Allegany River. The townspeople believed it to be cursed for any mortal who dared enter the mansion. From far away, the mansion was always visible. The mansion was dark and seemed to have been built many years ago, which made Leonardo wondered how it stood for so long. The castle was very old for its time, but to Leonardo's surprise, it seemed to blend in well with the town's architecture. Tall, spiked gates surrounded it, as if protecting the world from its treacherous inner demons. A humble, loyal servant opened the gate as Leonardo and Boris walked forward. Leonardo looked upon the servant and could hear the man's fear; his heart was pounding, and he was whispering a prayer under his breath, for the servant knew what they were. When their eyes met, the servant quickly looked down, trembling in fear. His past was filled with mischief and greed. The servant was a thief and was wanted for murder of eight innocent children. He had no honor, nor any dignity left in his heart. Leonardo felt ashamed and disgusted by this servant's wretched past. It seemed that Vampires would pick the most cowardice mortals to do their bidding. Leonardo quickly looked away and started to wonder what was waiting for him. Even if it was danger behind those doors, Leonardo hoped that he could find more answers. Following Lucius and Boris, he could hear wild dogs in the distance fighting over a dead dear that had been brought to them to feed on.

"Why are there dogs here?" Leonardo asked.

"Think of them as protectors during the daylight or, like many refer to them, as the hounds of hell," Lucius answered.

Hounds of hell, Leonardo thought.

"See, unlike mortals, they tend to obey their masters," Lucius explained.

The castle door graciously opened. The interior of the castle was nothing like Leonardo had ever seen. It was filled with artifacts and paintings he had never known of. The entire castle was dark to cover from the daylight, but it was decorated with distinguished, priceless heirlooms not from their century. Standing by a long, expanding staircase were the most beautiful creatures Leonardo had ever laid eyes on. There were four strong male vampires and five gorgeous female vampires. Boris and Lucius respectfully greeted them, as they were honored to be in their presence. Everyone seemed to behave with grace and caution; they hardly laughed or gave a smile, as humans normally would in such a special occasion. The female vampires, on the other hand, acted seductively. Some of them were dominant, with evil in their eyes, and others were caressing the male vampires by touching their long, sensual hair and stroking their chest and arms. It seemed to Leonardo that this was a common gesture of sexuality from the female vampires.

Standing in the entryway, Leonardo felt very small among the over-powering and confident vampires. He felt as if he was back in the forest, threatened by his surroundings. Leonardo was an amateur among them, with little knowledge of this new world he was now living in. So many unanswered questions made him fearful of knowing the truth. He realized that this made him vulnerable; he hid his emotions so that they would not be heard and used against him. Boris's voice interrupted his thoughts as he was asked to go to his side, *don't be afraid, Leonardo, come with me,* he said. As he was walking over, Leonardo felt all eyes on him, as he became the center of attention. Everyone knew that he was a new vampire in the making.

As Boris introduced Leonardo, most of them could sense Leonardo's troubled emotions. Some said that he was pathetic and different and that he would not last a whole century as a vampire, while others thought he was strong and beautiful and believed that there was something special about him.

"Leonardo, let me introduce you to some old friends of thy heart. Meet Carmina, Eva, Hendryk, and the wise Greguska."

"It's a pleasure," Leonardo replied respectively.

"Leonardo, what is your family name?" Eva asked.

"It's Le' Muerte, ma'am," Leonardo answered while Eva moved a strand of hair from his face.

"Looks like someone's manners are still intact. Intriguing," Carmina said as she approached him.

"I've never met such a unique vampire before," Eva added. "You are very different, Leonardo Le' Muerte."

As words were exchanged, Carmina came and stood next to Leonardo and began to lean toward the open area of his neck. Leonardo began to feel breathless, and a lustful desire clouded his mind. He couldn't resist what was going on within him. Visions began to form, that he, Carmina, and Eva were intertwined in each other's embrace. The more he felt their pleasures, the more he was giving into them.

"I just want a small taste, my love," Carmina whispered.

As she was about to place her spellbound lips on him, Boris pushed her away, shoving her into Hendryk. "You're not allowed to use your deceitful charms on Leonardo, Carmina. The next time will be your last. You have been warned," Boris said. Leonardo rapidly came to his senses from Carmina's manipulation. He had felt his cold blood boil under his skin, giving him the desire to take Carmina and fulfill wild sensual fantasies.

Carmina Ferreira was a young vampire, just about to reach the age of two hundred and twenty. She inherited a petite frame and blond lioness curls. She had a sense of fashion, as her brown dress hung on her body, bringing out her silver fox eyes and pale skin. Carmina had the gift of being able to manipulate those who were vulnerable. By releasing their sexual fantasies, she used her abilities to win her prey over to drain them of their blood and end their lives when she chose to.

On the other side of Carmina stood the beautiful four-hundred-year-old Parisian vampire, Eva Valleria. She chose her prey with careful precision, picking only wealthy men to feed on. Eva was provocative like the other female vampires, but her earthly brown eyes hid the bloody tales of her past. Her dark brown hair was combed back, barely touching her bare shoulders. Sparkling black diamonds hung from her neck, expressing the elegance of her black dress that brought out her curves. Her beauty and language, sought out by any man or vampire, gave way to her vicious history.

As for Hendryk and Greguska Kortig, they were five hundred and seventy-five-year-old German twins. They had almost the same characteristics. Both had the same calm blue eyes, and both dressed in their classic navy waistcoats with black satin breeches. Hendryk and Greguska had the ability to communicate with others by using telepathy. What made them different was the gift that they each possessed. Hendryk had the gift of seduction and knowledge. He was able to see the secrets of others and use them to manipulate them. Meanwhile, Greguska possessed the ability to move as fast as the blink of an eye. He also possessed the ability to block other vampires' abilities when threatened. Together, they were seen as a force to be reckoned with.

"On behalf of Greguska and me, we welcome you to the castle," Hendryk said as he straightened himself and stretched his hand out to Leonardo for a handshake.

Leonardo gave a nod of thanks with a cautionary smile as he shook Hendryk's hand.

"Leonardo, as you meet the rest of us, keep your emotions in control, for some of us might use it against you," Greguska said, standing a few feet away from his brother and drinking a glass of crimson blood.

Across the room, Lucius was speaking with the other six vampires: Nicholai Belhum and Uberto Crevier, both from Spain; Emon Gallager from Ireland; Viktoria Whittington and Rubia Theyer from England; and Nylora Antonescu from Romania. Each vampire had his or her own unique characteristics.

Nicholai and Uberto had been living for about six hundred years, but together they had history as old friends. Both were soldiers in the war, and both became vampires when attacked in their sleep. Nicholai had the gift of flight and movement like a spider along the walls. Uberto's gift was more unique then the others. He had the ability to shape shift into a werewolf, which aided him in killing his prey. Then there was Viktoria, who was four hundred and fifty-two years old. She was known for her reputation as one of the deadliest female vampires. She had a great thirst for any living thing, animal and human alike. Viktoria had beautiful, long, golden hair that brought out her emerald eyes. She had the look of a princess but a desire to kill anything or anyone that got in her way. As for Rubia, she was six hundred years old and was every man's desire. She inherited gorgeous, plump lips, beautiful purple eyes, and long, wild brown hair. All her features brought out her amazing sexuality. She carried herself with such elegance and confidence that even Leonardo fancied her. Rubia had a gentler soul, but behind her beauty, she was a danger to both mortal men and women. She would tempt them to sleep with her and then use them as puppets to do her bidding, and once the pleasure was over, she would slaughter them and drink their blood until their miserable lives ended. Then there was Nylora; she was the quietest of the group of vampires in the room. However, everyone knew that it was the quiet ones you had to keep an eye on. Her slim figure and her coal-black hair allowed her to attack her enemies in the shadows. She was only ninety-two years old, but she was trained by her master to move among the shadows yet cause agonizing pain, as if it was her last night to be an immortal. Standing next to Nylora was Emon, who was once a great nobleman in Ireland, until he was turned into a vampire during the Dark Ages. From the knowledge by his maker and his time as a nobleman, Emon created his image to be that of a leader and not another follower. Not even a week had passed since being turned into a vampire before he secretly tortured and killed his maker, knowing well that it was against the vampire ways. Only few vampires, including Boris, knew about the incident, for they all knew that if the other vampire covenants found out, it would result in sudden death. Emon had killed many mortals over the decades, more than he could count. From the way he grew to be, Emon was admired as one of the most feared yet respected vampires in their covenant. He was seen as an extremely fearless force amongst the immortals.

By 1598, each of the nine vampires appeared in each other's lives, and became members of the Dominus covenant, founded in Rome, 304 A.D. by Romulus. From the first era of the covenant, the previous members were sent to join forces with other vampire covenants around the world to attend their council. Throughout the centuries of the first era, the covenant was filled with power, loyalty, hatred, and betrayal. In spite of their imperfections, the covenant remained as a greater supremacy toward the rest of the vampire covenants. Whispers and voices filled the void of the castle as the newborn vampire in the room distracted almost everyone.

"Who is your friend, Lucius?" Nicholai asked as he turned his back against the introductions and walked with Lucius into the main dining hall where Rubia, Viktoria, Uberto, and Emon were standing.

"He is not with me; he is no one that I've met before," Lucius replied while drinking a fresh cup of blood.

"Then why is he here?" Nicholai asked, eyeing Leonardo from a distance.

"He seems so sorrowful, pathetic, and so out of place, yet he is filled with so much pain inside. That's what makes him so fascinating," Rubia said, approaching Lucius and Nicholai from behind.

"It seems that his name is Leonardo Le' Muerte," Lucius replied. "A vampire with unbearable issues that I don't care to comprehend."

"There is so much beauty and compassion in his eyes, and he is so handsome. Why wouldn't you want to understand a creature like that?" Viktoria asked Lucius.

"What are you saying, Viktoria?" Nicholai replied with a sense of jealousy. "We all know that the only reason you crave him is for your own pleasure. He is an infant compared to us."

"He does not belong here. He should have stayed as a worthless mortal living among the lifeless world," said Uberto.

"He has power and beauty, but most of all, he is humble. These are things that you, Uberto, fail to learn and understand," Rubia said, standing next to Viktoria, both mesmerized by Leonardo.

"How dare you compare him with me?" Uberto said. "He is an insignificant insect among a web of spiders."

"Should we ask them to leave, Lucius?" Emon said as he stood with his arms crossed.

"No, Emon. Let us give them a chance to prove that Leonardo is like one of us," Lucius replied.

Mixed attitudes toward Leonardo were becoming more noticeable. Leonardo knew that he had to prove himself and show that his emotions, thoughts, and individuality were no harm to their covenant. He had no special gifts, which made him realize that being accepted would be a more difficult task than he thought.

As it became apparent to him that he was being watched, Leonardo felt defenseless in their presence, wishing he had the ability to hear their thoughts. He excused himself from the group of vampires who were gossiping and analyzing him and began to walk over to the lavish living room where the whispers of the vampires gradually faded away and the crackle of the fireplace consumed the room. Leonardo sat next to the fireplace, feeling the warmth of the burning fire. It was the closest feeling he could remember compared to the intensity of the sun.

Suddenly, Leonardo realized that he was not alone. A shadow appeared from the corner of the room, forming the figure of a woman. She had a petite frame, one that could fool any man, considering the vampire strength she possessed. Her eyes were brown with a shade of honey, which was brought out by her long brown hair that was braided to the side, caressing her heart-shaped face. She was wearing a white dress, decorated by brown ribbons and laced, ruffled sleeves. She was unusually beautiful. Nevertheless, Leonardo wondered why she was alone and not with the others. She didn't seem like the others, who attempted to seduce him. As Leonardo's eyes met hers, he began to feel her suffering and hatred of how she had to live her life in the darkness. With curiosity lingering in the air, Leonardo introduced himself. He knew that she was curious as well, and with some hesitation, she finally introduced herself. Her name was Ilene Welbeck; she had just celebrated her one hundred and six-fifth birthday a couple of weeks ago.

As Ilene stared into Leonardo's eyes, she could see the trust that they could possibly share. She began to let Leonardo see what she wanted him to see through her eyes. Flashes of her beginning invaded his mind, intruding his own thoughts as if he was there in person, witnessing her story. She came from a small town in Virginia and was known by many as the beautiful daughter of the town's mayor. However, due to the power that her father held, many men desired her, until one night she was kidnapped and went missing for days. Rumors spread throughout the town, that because of her innocent beauty, she had been raped many times by various power-hungry men. Yet, no one really knew what really happened during her disappearance. Weeks later, she found her way back home as a newborn vampire. Her thirst for blood was so unbearable that she only remembered waking up the next night with blood covering the entire town. As Ilene was telling her story through telepathy, shame appeared across her face. Ilene looked away and became quiet. She stared down at her hands and began to fidget with her ring. It was a stunning gold ring, encrusted with deep blue sapphires and diamonds; a ring of value that her father had given to her when she was a little girl.

Leonardo could not help but sympathize with her pain. "My own family was slaughtered when I just a boy. I lost my sister and my own way of life. I am deeply sorry for your loss," Leonardo said, feeling sorry for her.

"So am I. We both come from a world of loss and cruelty. We both loved our families. You loved your sister as much as I loved my father," Ilene replied.

"What happened to your father?" he asked. "If you don't mind me asking, that is."

On the other side of the room, Lucius could not help but notice the connection that Ilene and Leonardo were forming. Using his abilities, Lucius intruded into Leonardo's mind to find out what they were saying. As he listened closely, he realized that Leonardo was developing an interest in Ilene; he wanted to know more about how she became who she was.

Children will be children, Lucius thought.

"I do not like him," Emon projected to Lucius.

"Neither do I, Emon," Lucius replied. "But he is Boris's problem; let him deal with this boy, not us."

"If you change your mind, let me know, and I will deal with him myself," Emon said, cracking his neck slowly from side to side.

"Everything disturbs you, Emon," Viktoria said. "Romulus would not allow it unless Leonardo defies us."

"Viktoria is right. Without cause, we cannot kill the boy," Lucius said while taking another sip of blood from his glass. "We will have to wait and see how their destiny will unfold."

As everyone waited patiently for the arrival of Romulus, the head of the covenant, a wave of silence came throughout the castle, and all heads turned toward the marble, winding staircase. Leonardo looked over to see what caused the silence. He then turned to Ilene to get answers, but she had suddenly vanished.

* * * *

Romulus Vandesius, one of the most fearful and respected elder vampires known in the world, leader of the vampire councils, founder of the Dominus covenant, and creator of the Vampyr laws, gracefully came down the stairs. Romulus had on a silk white dress shirt that peeked through his maroon and silver, laced banyan coat, accompanied by black breeches and custom leather shoes. The way he dressed was like no man Leonardo had ever seen. Everyone that knew Romulus knew that he was a serious man. His figure was slim with features of a man in his late twenties. His right hand was adorned with a gold ring with a red ruby, which had been passed down to him from other ancients before him as a sign of leadership. Romulus had the most daring light gray eyes that could easily seduce any mortal or immortal with one glance. Throughout the centuries of existence as a vampire, Romulus came to embrace unbelievable abilities and gifts along the way. He had the gift of healing faster than any other immortal; however, he was more known for the ability that allowed him to take a person's emotions and elevate them to hysterical heights that ushered them into reality. In other words, Romulus had the power to turn one's fear and use it against them. Hence, in his long reign, there hadn't been any immortal that dared to challenge his rule.

The gorgeous vampire Tabitha Giordano accompanied him. She was reaching the age of seven hundred and seventy-one. Born in Lavinium, Italy, she was known as one of the eldest female vampires in the era, as well as cruel and deceitful. Tabitha had a desire to feed on young mortals that had a taste for cruelty and committing adultery. Nevertheless, she was a sight to be seen; her appearance was decorated by years of collected lace and jewels that represented her power. Tabitha came down the stairs, flowing with a long-sleeved, black, European chemise dress that showed off her robust, stunning body. What made her stand out most was her diamond-studded, black birdcage veil that bestowed a shadow over her beautiful features.

Tabitha and Romulus joined everyone, and Tabitha graciously gave a grand welcome to all for coming at such short notice. As Romulus made his way around, he walked toward Boris with great pleasure and curiosity.

"I thought you had disappeared, Boris. I am deeply touched to see you once again, my friend," said Romulus.

"It is nice to see you again too, Romulus, as always," Boris replied with a friendly smile.

While Romulus continued greeting the other vampires, Boris and Tabitha's eyes met. Boris was surprised to see his maker after all these decades. Tabitha was also surprised to see him. She centered her attention only on Boris and no one else in the room.

"My fallen angel," she said as she approached him.

"Tabitha," Boris replied as he kissed her delicate hands with grace.

"You have changed so much, Boris. I feel it greatly, and I must say it pleases me to see how much power and wisdom you have gained."

"You have not changed as well and are still gorgeous from last time we gathered."

"Yes, indeed, Boris. It is a pleasure to have you with us, Tabitha," Carmina said as she walked past them and approached Romulus.

"No, my dear, the pleasure is all mine," Tabitha, responded without taking her eyes from Boris.

Tabitha's eyes then glided over from Boris to Leonardo.

"Who is this?" she asked.

Boris knew exactly whom she was asking about, but before he could answer her, Boris waited for brief moment until Romulus was occupied with Lucius and the rest of the vampires.

"His name is Leonardo Le' Muerte, and I am his maker."

Tabitha's curiosity began to blossom. She stared at Leonardo for a moment, easily able to feel his troubled emotions.

"Leonardo," she said, playing the name around upon her lips. "There is something unusual about him, something that I can't understand."

"What do you mean?" Boris asked.

"As knowledgeable as you have become, Boris, you cannot read more than what you see, can you?" Tabitha said. "We shall talk before dawn, and I will show you what you do not see."

From among the crowd, Eva, Carmina, and Hendryk could not resist joining in the whispers going around about Leonardo.

"You just can't deny how irresistibly tasteful he looks," Eva said, glancing toward Leonardo. "Don't you agree, Carmina?"

"I truly agree with you, Eva. I just wish I was his maker; I would have so much fun with him," Carmina replied.

"I believe he will become a great elder one day. I can see the power that he withholds. Leonardo possesses greater potential than any other newborn I've ever encountered. But he must first learn the ways in which we live as vampires; if not, he will be lost and possibly become an easy hunt for others," Hendryk chimed in.

Romulus had welcomed everyone; he announced that the formal gathering would take place in the grand dining hall. As all the elders, including Lucius, began following Romulus, Leonardo got up and started his way alongside Boris, but Boris stopped him as he placed his hand firmly on his shoulder.

"Only the elders and masters of this covenant are allowed to attend this gathering, Leonardo."

"Why? Am I not one of you?" Leonardo asked.

"You are still a newborn vampire. In time, you will know everything and what will be asked from you."

"I understand."

"In the meantime, have fun. Enjoy yourself and feel free to wander around the castle. Just don't get too lost. If you do, don't worry. Atticus will find you."

"Who's Atticus?" Leonardo asked.

"He is what you would call a historian. Trust me—you will find him quite intriguing yet very helpful."

Understanding that Leonardo had much to learn, Boris turned and left to join the rest of the covenant in the dining hall.

As everyone disappeared and left to mind their own business, Leonardo realized that he was alone in the entryway of the mansion. He turned around and began to wander among the foreign surroundings. Standing alone in the middle of the room, the castle felt massive. Looking above, Leonardo was captivated by the innocent angels painted within the dome of the ceiling. Suspended from the center of the concaved ceiling was a grand French empire chandelier. The fire flickering from each candlestick arranged around the chandelier illuminated each crystal. Leonardo had never seen such beauty come from such detailed architecture. Every wall, column, and the vast winding staircase were engraved with old Romanian carvings, luxuriously covered in gold. Truly, Leonardo began to believe that the Dominus covenant was the most powerful of all.

Curious to see what was beyond, Leonardo headed up the marble stairway. With each step he took, Leonardo was mesmerized by the collection of priceless treasurers that decorated the grand castle. Reaching the second floor, his path split between the east and west wing, each going down a dark path that was only lit by the candled lanterns hanging on the wall. Leonardo chose to go down the west wing, cautious of the darkness and the mystery that might lie ahead. With his senses heightened, he walked past closed doors and large, ancient portraits of men and women in various types of clothing. Each portrait represented different eras in history, but what was common from the paintings was that there seemed to be dark-cloaked figures painted in some of them. The dark figures expressed extreme mystery in the background of the paintings as they stared at the main painted figure in the foreground. Something eerie about these paintings began to draw Leonardo's attention to take a closer look. Unexpectedly, Leonardo heard from afar a strange wind blowing through a cracked door. He gradually approached the door; curious about what lay behind the malice and evil castle—when abruptly all the haunting air began to suffocate Leonardo. What he witnessed behind the door gave truth to the newborn monster that now lived within him.

VIII

In the windowless room were rows of beds that were each occupied with a human body. Leonardo could sense that some were on the verge of death, as others were freshly plucked from the outside world and put into this horrifying room. They each were in a deep sleep as the needles in their arms slowly drained the blood from their bodies. Leonardo's eyes followed the path of each line of blood that poured into a heated spherical orb built into the wall. Some of the bodies seemed to twitch every so often, as if they were experiencing horrible nightmares with no way to be released from them. It was one of the most horrifying things he has ever seen. As Leonardo was trying to leave, he stumbled into another room in the mansion. The bedroom was not set like any ordinary room; it was simple yet elegant and contained only the needs of a vampire. In the middle of the room lay a large Persian rug, and in the far corner sat a piano. Across from the piano, a whole wall was dedicated to a wide selection of books from all over the world. However, what caught Leonardo's attention the most about the room was that in the center of it all was a coffin. Everything revolved around this one object. Leonardo didn't know what to think. The mysteries were yet to be discovered, and the questions he had were yet to be answered, but Leonardo knew that one day he would know everything.

Leonardo left the room, trying to be discrete as he continued to walk down the hallway. Keeping his head down, he stumbled upon another dark hallway where he began to hear a distant voice within the air. He followed the disembodied voice until finally he reached the end of the hallway. Suddenly, it occurred to Leonardo that he had ended up stepping into some kind of dungeon that was lit by dimly lit lanterns that hung along the walls. Within the dungeon, he could see a tall, scrawny-looking man. Shorter than he was, the man had long brown hair that had not been brushed in years. He wore old, ragged clothes and sandals that looked outdated. The man appeared to be caring for an ill dog that was chained down at the edge of the dungeon. This man didn't appear to be a vampire, or even a possible threat to him. It simply looked as if he was one of Romulus's mortal slaves that cleaned and watched over the castle during the daytime.

"Excuse me," Leonardo said.

The man startled and turned around to look at him.

"Oh my, no matter how long I've been among you, I still don't seem to get used to that."

"I am sorry if I startled you."

"Sorry?" the man asked in confusion. "That's a first. Hardly any vampire that has lived in this castle has ever apologized. You must be a really fascinating newborn vampire, because I believe you are, my lord."

"You're not a vampire, yet you seem to know a lot about us. Who are you?"

"My name is Atticus, the record keeper of the vampires."

"A record keeper?" Leonardo wondered as he took a step toward the man. "How did you get involved in all this?"

"It's a long story," Atticus replied, "Correct me if I am wrong, my lord, but are you the one they call Leonardo?"

"I am."

"It's a great honor to meet you, Leonardo," Atticus said kindly, bowing his head slightly forward, as if honoring him in some way.

Atticus stared into Leonardo's eyes for a moment and felt that he was indeed different. He couldn't fully explain it in words, but he could sense that Leonardo possessed an extraordinary willpower that resided within him. Atticus had never seen such a creature that seemed to value and understand life as Leonardo did.

"What are you seeking, my lord?" Atticus asked. "You seem to be searching for something. Am I right?"

Surprised at how much the man knew, Leonardo couldn't stop the words from coming out of his mouth. "I am searching for what I lost a long time ago," Leonardo replied as he looked upon the ill dog. "I am also searching for answers about what I have become. There has to be an understanding to all this madness."

"You sure are different from many other newborns that I have come across, my lord." Atticus said, "I don't know much about the beginning of your kind, but I can do my best to answer some of your questions that I am permitted to. Follow me."

Leonardo followed Atticus out of the dungeon and down into another dark hallway that led up to a small tower within the castle. He wondered what Atticus could possibly show him and if it was truly going to answer his questions.

Maybe these are secrets that Boris kept to himself. Or are these answers that many vampires sought and were killed for knowing too much? Leonardo thought.

Anxious to finally hear the truth behind this monstrous, dark underworld, they arrived at a single door at the very top of the tower. Atticus opened the door, but as he was about to step into the room, he invited Leonardo to go in first, "Please, come in my lord." Cautiously walking inside, he could smell the aroma of old paper and melted candles. They seemed to walk into a vast library. Enormous shelves consumed either side of the room, and within the shelves were various books of different sizes. On the tables were rolled parchment and articles, and all along the walls were old paintings of vampires from different centuries.

"What is this place?" Leonardo asked, looking upon the many books.

"This is where Lord Romulus keeps all of the vampire records. Every story, every vampire that ever lived, and every murder that ever occurred—it has all been kept here. Even the myths, legends, folktales, prophecies, everything that any mortal ever considered to be false, this is the room to find out the truth," Atticus said

"Really? Within these records and books, I will certainly find my answers?" Leonardo asked.

"Well, not all. Lord Romulus made sure that not all stories are kept here for any wandering peasant or unwelcomed vampire to steal or read upon."

"What can you tell me about the origins of the vampires?"

"I don't know much about the origins of the vampires, but I do know that you were all created many thousands of years ago."

"Created? By whom?" Leonardo asked.

"Let's just say that 'The Cursed' have existed unnoticed throughout humankind's history. Not many mortals have seen them, but they have played a huge role in the history of man. Again, I don't know too much about them; Lord Romulus keeps most of the story undisclosed."

"I see. It's just as I feared; there seems more to it than I imagined. Yet I thought we were the only ones living in this world," Leonardo said.

"Oh, you have no idea. There are more foul creatures in the shadows than vampires. At least vampires like to keep themselves civilized. I would tell you more about them, but I am afraid that Lord Romulus will have me bled dry if I did. He has powers beyond comprehension."

"I understand," Leonardo replied. "But how did you manage to survive for centuries? Clearly you don't possess any powers."

"A long time ago, in ancient Roman times, I was chosen by Lord Romulus to be his record keeper. At the time, I believed it to be a great honor to have been chosen, but there was a prize to pay. I have been drinking his blood in order to be immortal just like you. I never age or die from sickness, and as long as I drink his blood, I am cursed with immortality. Unfortunately, the only difference is that I can be killed like any mortal, and unlike a true vampire, I can walk in the sunlight, but I can never be as I was before."

"Why haven't you tried to flee from him?" Leonardo asked.

"I have tried countless times, there was even a time when I believed in such a thing called freedom. Yet, I am bound to Lord Romulus. This curse keeps my soul chained to his, until death should find me."

"Are there others like you?"

"Yes," Atticus replied. "Each of the seven vampire covenants in the world has their own record keeper in order to document everything that has happened. Like mortals have their own history, vampires like to have theirs."

"If all this is true, and there are far worse things that I can't fully comprehend yet, then why does it seem that I am different from the others?" Leonardo asked as he gently squeezed the edge of one of the bookshelves, almost breaking the entire bookshelf.

"I know this world must be hell for you, my lord, feeling that you have enemies in every corner, waiting to see you fail. But keep this in mind: you are a newborn unlike any other. When I see you, I don't see another lost soul like the rest of us. I see hope and light somewhere within you. You have the power to decide what kind of immortal you want to become. Whether you believe it or not, the choice is still yours."

Leonardo felt confused and a range of emotions. There was more to it than he had anticipated and trying to get his questions answered created more questions still waiting to be answered. Leonardo stared blankly at the books and the old articles, as if all of the mysteries were waiting to unfold. Curiosity seemed to diminish as Atticus's words came into his mind: *this is who you are, and this is all that you will ever be.*

There was nothing else he could think of to ask Atticus, so Leonardo decided to leave the room and head back into the dark halls, continuing his speculations about what he had heard from Atticus. Leonardo knew there was more to it. Yet, for now, it seemed that there was no way out, and nowhere to go to but to keep on walking until someone took him away from the long and infinite misery of the darkness that surrounded him.

As he walked the path that lay ahead, what he had become for eternity was unendurable. He could not bear the truth. He felt darkness crushing him and the need to get out of the castle. Overwhelmed with all his thoughts and the rooms that occupied the mansion, he headed back toward the main staircase and caught a glimpse of a figure.

Ilene? Leonardo wondered.

Recognizing the brown, braided hair of Ilene, he followed her through a narrow hallway between two statues of gargoyles. As she swiftly turned the corner to her left, he followed her to a large terrace that overlooked the dark forest and beyond. He turned to face Ilene, but before he could ask her about the rooms he had witnessed earlier, she disappeared without a word. Leonardo walked over to the edge of the terrace, amazed to see the vast lands of Pittsburgh with the beauty of the stars stretching out over the mountains. Never in his lifetime had he seen such a remarkable sight. Feeling the gentle breeze of the night wind, all his worries seemed to vanish. All his troubles about his new life and everything that he had foreseen seemed to subside within the darkness.

I never would have thought this world held so much mystery and immortal wickedness, Leonardo thought.

Moments later, Leonardo looked down from the terrace to see the elders exiting the front door, waiting for their chariots to arrive. As he saw them from above, he began to observe the way they spoke, their body language, and each of their distinctive characteristics. From behind, a soft voice brought him out of his thoughts.

"Peculiar, isn't it?" Ilene said.

"What is?" Leonardo replied as he turned around to face her.

"The way in which we vampires must live." She stated, as she walked over to stand beside him.

Is she talking about the rooms? Leonardo wondered.

"In this world, there are not too many secrets that can be kept from us. Enduring the amount of work needed to keep that secret is very tiresome," Ilene said. "Like the attendance of your presence. Boris knew he couldn't keep you to himself forever."

"I should not be surprised. In one night, everyone has come to learn who I am. But as a human slave, the world didn't care to know who I was, dying each day."

Ilene turned and looked at him with understanding in her eyes. "You are no longer that slave, my dear Leonardo. You are an immortal now, and you and I are more alike than you think."

"How so?"

"Decades ago, after I was turned by my maker at the age of twenty-two, I killed the one person that mattered to me. He taught me everything I knew and loved me as no other man had loved a daughter."

"You murdered your father?" Leonardo replied; shocked at why she would do such a thing to a person she loved.

"I had no choice, Leonardo. My maker, the demon who brought me back, forced me. I did not want to do it, believe me; I loved my father very much. As you now understand, the thirst overpowered my love for him. I have been living with regret all these years. He was my father, but now I just remember him as my first victim," Ilene explained, with the memory lingering in her mind. "Had I known of this life as a mortal being, I wouldn't wish it on my worst enemy."

"If you hate being what you are, why are you still here?"

"I would rather choose to burn under the sun, if it wasn't for the forced laws of the Vampyr."

"It seems that I am not the only one forced into this lifestyle. I cannot imagine having to follow forced laws, nor can I imagine the pain of dying from the one thing that brings life into this world," Leonardo stated, feeling pity for her.

"Interesting. Now I see why the others are so attracted to you, Leonardo, and it is not because of your charms," she replied with a shy smile as she glanced at him.

"What do you mean?"

"You possess something that is very rare in a vampire, Leonardo. You hold the ability to feel emotion. When one becomes a vampire like us, everything is switched off. Our feelings and emotions are as cold as our pale skin and set like our cold heart. So, the fact that you are able to feel means that your heart is strong, that you still have some light left in you."

"Light? Ilene, at the age of ten, I witnessed my family's death and had to endure the loss of everyone that I loved. I've been a slave for a ruthless man for seven years, and now I'm this," Leonardo explained. "Now we are creatures that are cursed to last forever, without redemption or salvation for our souls."

"I believe everyone has their own will to choose, Leonardo. It is just matter of letting go what you have lost. Doing so will present the true beauty of being an immortal."

"I don't think I will ever see the true beauty of it."

"Come with me," Ilene said, grabbing his hand off the railing of the terrace and pulling him back into the hallway.

As they were walking back into the darkness of the hallway, and before Leonardo could ask where Ilene was taking him, Romulus appeared before them.

"What a pleasant surprise to see you both here. However, your presence was greatly missed at the gathering, Ilene," Romulus said as he approached them with a subtle smile.

"I did not know that my attendance was needed, Romulus. I apologize," Ilene responded, showing the utmost respect toward him.

"Your apology is accepted, my dear. Now, would you mind leaving us for a moment? I would like a word with Leonardo."

Ilene looked at Leonardo, concerned by what Romulus would talk to him about. She left the hallway with her head down as Romulus and Leonardo headed back toward the terrace. Ilene promised herself that she would try to convince Leonardo to escape the Vampyr world with her.

With the cool breeze blowing toward the land, Romulus walked past Leonardo and leaned against the aged railing, watching the trees and the dark sky of the night.

"Let me properly introduce myself. I am Romulus Vandesius, and I know who you are, Leonardo Le' Muerte."

"It's a pleasure to meet you, sir."

"The pleasure is all mine, Leonardo."

With the wind blowing through the trees and the night owl crying out, moments passed before any more words were exchanged between Romulus and Leonardo.

"Living the many years that I have lived, only then can you really understand the beauty of the night," Romulus said while he inhaled the freshness of the air.

"I wouldn't know anything about that; I barely comprehend the meaning of all of this," Leonardo said. "I mean, how did vampires come into this world? Why did you create the laws of the Vampyr, and why must we follow them? Why are we the way we are?"

"You have many questions for someone so young. I know Atticus spoke to you, and I know he told you what you needed to hear. With time, you will get all the answers you seek."

"I would like to know the truth, and I think you can tell me what I need to know."

"If you want your questions to be answered, why not ask your maker?" Romulus suggested as he turned to acknowledge Leonardo, his head turned to one side.

As if it was so simple, Leonardo thought.

"Boris wants me to accept the present, to accept who I am and let go of my past," Leonardo responded. "I understand that he is my maker and that he has given me a new life. How can I trust someone who will not give me a reason for why I am still alive? How can I understand this world when I am to follow the laws of the Vampyr without any explanation?"

Romulus thought for a moment. "The laws of the Vampyr were created to protect the vampire species. To understand this life, you have to remember one thing. As you are now a vampire, fear is nonexistent in our world, because now the world fears us. Letting go of your past will help you understand this, Leonardo."

My past is what gives me purpose, Leonardo told himself.

"How can we live in this world as monsters when we are the last people to deserve salvation for killing the innocent?" Leonardo replied.

"The man who enslaved you wasn't very innocent, Leonardo. We are not the monsters, my dear friend. We are the greatest and most powerful immortals that have ever ruled this planet. We rejoice in the sins of the people and make them into our sanctuary. As mortals may live their lives with a conscience, we as vampires live with none," Romulus explained further.

Understanding the difference between mortals and immortals, Leonardo became concerned about the consequences an immortal had to live with if they defied the ways of a vampire.

"Being one of the oldest vampires, I've only heard tales, before my time, of selfish and arrogant ancients living as gods and monsters. For centuries, since the laws have existed because of me, there has never been a vampire who opposed my ruling of secrecy," Romulus continued, answering Leonardo's unspoken question. "If there were such a vampire to oppose us, they would be judged by their elders, given permission by me and the Dominus. The most serious judgment that would fall upon a vampire would be death by their first and last sunrise. Their names would be erased from our history, to never be spoken of again."

Leonardo was beginning to understand everything Romulus explained to him; however, he began to feel that Romulus knew more than what he was attempting to explain. Leonardo searched within Romulus's eye for an answer.

On the other hand, Romulus knew that Leonardo was searching for answers about his family and the tragedy that had befallen them, but he knew that Leonardo was not ready to know the truth. Romulus decided to distract him with another issue at hand.

"Leonardo, there is something that you need to know about Boris."

Disappointed that Romulus did not reveal what he was hiding, Leonardo was concerned about his maker.

"Boris is planning on leaving you," Romulus stated.

"Why would he do that?"

"He will join back with his maker, Tabitha. It is amazing how after so many years apart, it only took a few moments for them to make up their minds. Tabitha is trying to convince Boris to kill you because it seems you are caught in the middle. The one thing that is holding Boris back is you. He does not want to kill you because he believes that you will be useful to him."

Leonardo was confused and unsure of why Romulus was telling him this. He wondered for a minute if the reason Romulus was telling him to leave was to protect his own covenant. Again, as if Romulus was reading Leonardo's thoughts, he answered, "You are one of us, and therefore I consider you as my son. As a father, I suggest you leave Boris; it is the best thing you can do for yourself, Leonardo." Romulus placed both hands on Leonardo's shoulders. "There is much to be gained if you decide to leave your maker, Leonardo.

You have a gift that could benefit this covenant, and I'd rather you stay and learn —"

"Then why can't you do anything about it?" Leonardo asked, taking a step back from Romulus as he interrupted him.

Briefly closing his eyes and taking a deep breath, Romulus explained that by the laws of the Vampyr, he could not stand between a maker and their protégé. That was a choice to be made between them, to separate according to their vow to one another.

It seemed that Leonardo's only way of survival with this second life that he was given was to run. There was simply no other option.

⁎   ⁎   ⁎   ⁎

Far across the castle, Boris was standing in the middle of the vast library. The growing collection of the books was said to have dated back to the very first vampires who ever roamed the lands. Rumors said that the history written in these books became the way it was because of the fight to keep vampires a secret from the world. Contemplating the journey that might take place and the decisions that had to be made, Boris began to doubt himself. Normally, Boris had few doubts. He lived his life in the moment, with no guilt or remorse. Beginning to pace back and forth, hovering along the bookshelves, Boris felt a sudden presence in the room.

As he turned around, he knew exactly who had entered. Tabitha was browsing through a book about the history and anatomy of newborn vampires. Noticing Boris's stare, she gracefully closed the book and placed it back on the shelf, and then she finally looked up to acknowledge him. With every step she took toward Boris, his hatred for her grew. He knew that every time they rekindled their relationship, she would abandon him the next day without a word. The problem was that he never could resist her.

Tabitha knew exactly what Boris was feeling as she looked at him with lust and desire. When she brought her hand up to caress Boris's face, he quickly grabbed her wrist and pushed her away.

"What do you want, Tabitha?" Boris asked.

"Oh, my dear, dear Boris," Tabitha responded as she stepped back to look at how beautiful and fierce he had become over the decades of being alone. "To see how much power you have gained greatly impresses me."

"No. You left me. I did not leave you. Our relationship was over when you last abandoned me many decades ago."

"I know. I am truly sorry for leaving you," she replied with just a glimpse of regret.

"I remember how you treated me before, Tabitha, like a puppet—toying and controlling me only for your pleasure. I was nothing to you, just someone you took advantage of," Boris said, trying not to be distracted by her gorgeous, full lips.

"Let's not reminisce about the past, Boris. I never meant to hurt you. Let us leave this wretched place together to make up for lost time. I want you more than ever to be by my side." Tabitha moved toward Boris, knowing well enough that her passion was distracting his anger.

"What about Leonardo?" he asked.

"Leave him. He is unworthy to be one of us; you would lose too much for his cause," Tabitha said as she ran her hand through his hair.

He is not worthy to have you, Tabitha whispered within his thoughts.

Boris looked at her with such temptation that he could not bear to resist her beauty. He looked away and walked over toward one of the windows, thinking about the offer that Tabitha just laid out for him—leaving Leonardo to go back to those days that he wanted with Tabitha so long ago. Yet he was afraid of the consequences he might face with Romulus and the covenant. He realized that even though Leonardo had disappointed him several times since he had been given his immortality, as his maker, there was a bond that he could not break. Nevertheless, the bond with Tabitha was much stronger. Boris couldn't deny his secret passion to have her once more in his arms, desiring to be hers for all time.

"Come with me and stay with me, my love," Tabitha whispered seductively against his ear as she suddenly appeared behind him.

Boris did not know what to do. For the first time since he had grown to become wise and powerful, he was stuck between two paths.

Tabitha did not want Boris to say no to her. With her alluring, sensual body, she walked around to face him with her hands upon his arms, feeling the growing tension of his muscles. Remembering the language of his body, she moved her hands toward his chest and down his torso, feeling every carved line of his body. She then leaned in for a kiss, and to her surprise, he did not hesitate. He was bound to her.

Boris began to feel the passion burn through his cold skin and upon her full lips.

As their lips were locked and their tongues were passionately intertwined, Boris knew well enough that he had the upper hand. He grabbed her arms and slammed her against the wall. The intense desire of his actions cracked the wall. Her hands moved against his arms to relieve the intensity of his strength so that she could be in control, but he would not back down. All the days that Boris had longed for with Tabitha began to surface, and he was not going to let her take that away. His hands moved down her body, feeling every curve and perfection as she moaned for his touch. Boris grabbed a hold of her legs and wrapped them around his waist. Pushing himself against her, the wall began to crumble beneath them.

Just as Boris was burying himself in Tabitha as he continued his kisses down to her throat, Leonardo was walking down the hallway approaching the doorway of the library.

"What is your answer, Boris? Will you stay with me?" Tabitha asked as her moans echoed in the air.

Boris pulled away from her, looking into her eyes for a moment, and finally said yes. Suddenly, Tabitha kissed him with an obsession; Boris had fallen right into her hands again.

As if the world was on her side, Leonardo heard what Boris agreed to as he was standing behind the closed door of the library. Confusion, hatred, and despair ran through Leonardo's mind, feeling that he was once again being abandoned. He was going to be alone again; the only difference now was that he would be living within the dark shadows of the overbearing moon. He could not believe what he was hearing. His maker, the one who had given him life for the second time, was going back to his maker. Romulus was right.

With every moan and whisper echoing in the library, Leonardo felt betrayed. He believed that Boris was his mentor, his guide into this unknown world. He had hoped to fill that hole in his heart that his family once occupied. Clearly, he was wrong. It seemed to Leonardo that Boris never saw anything in him; he was only another puppet of this world, just as Mr. Cooper and his own father treated him. For a moment full of hatred and pain, he wanted to barge into the library, and kill them both. Instead, Leonardo caught himself from going in. He knew that no matter how hard he fought, he would be outmatched by his maker and his maker's lover. The only way Leonardo knew he was going to survive was to run away. He ran through the halls and back into the main hallway. As Leonardo was running, he could hear whispers and daunting laughter echoing in every direction, as if they were chasing after him. Passing by Ilene, he had hoped they would be leaving together, but he knew he could not put her at risk with the elders for his troubles.

Ilene wanted to stop Leonardo from running, but she knew that the anger was too great within him because his eyes showed a thirst for blood and vengeance, a sight that terrified her.

Leonardo finally got outside and through the gates and was now far away from the distant castle. Even with the covenant far behind, Leonardo continued to run. He knew he had to find a place to stay hidden, as the sun was soon going to rise for a new day.

✳   ✳   ✳   ✳

Back at the terrace, Romulus was able to hear everything that was happening between Boris and Tabitha. He even knew that Leonardo ran away, just as he had encouraged him to. While the cold night breeze ran through his long hair, Romulus was at ease with what had just occurred because everything was happening just as he had planned.

IX

Leonardo ran as far as he could within the woods, hoping to free himself from the darkness that was growing inside. In the distance, he heard a traveler coming down the abandoned road, heading in his direction. Leonardo hid behind a tree, watching as his thirst for blood began to heighten. Watching the traveler heading toward the south of Pittsburgh, Leonardo knew that he could kill the man and take over the carriage, but he decided that the man's life was less important than the strength he needed to survive. With the limited amount of strength that Leonardo had, he jumped in the back of the empty carriage to hide from the coming sun.

Throughout the passage to his unknown destination, Leonardo looked up into the dark and misty night sky, listening to the owls in the trees and the wolves' howls echoing within the mountains. Contemplating what he had learned and experienced in the last few days with Boris and the Dominus covenant, he now had to plan his future to find the answers he was seeking and to find the truth behind his sister's whereabouts.

Leonardo began to figure out his next move when the carriage stopped at a small village. The drunken traveler wobbled off from the carriage and greeted an elderly man walking out from a nearby house.

"Thank goodness you made it, Jack! I thought you would never make it here on time!" the elderly man exclaimed.

"Sorry, sir. It was hard to see within the mist of the woods," Jack stated as he took a quick drink from his bourbon-filled flask.

"Did you bring the money?"

"Am I not a man of my word?" Jack replied.

"I guess we shall see," the elderly man responded with a stern gaze.

Suddenly they were both startled by a noise from the back of the carriage. The man and Jack were both alarmed and guarded, thinking that someone might be spying on them and catching them in the act of trading stolen money. The man glanced from Jack to the back of the carriage, hoping not to find someone lurking about in their business. Walking slowly with hesitating steps, Jack pulled his gun from his side, ready to fire at the undesired witness. With his mind racing through the possible ways of how he could get rid of the body, Jack grabbed the handle of the carriage and pulled the door open. There was no one there.

"What are you playing at?" the man yelled. "Are you trying to make me question our business together?"

"What are you so worried about?" Jack asked. "Anyone who would come in between our business would wish that they never did."

"I hope so," the man said.

After escaping from the carriage, Leonardo walked through the slumbering village, trying to find a place to hide before his thirst took control. He made his way, acknowledging the houses and shops that took up the unfamiliar small village. The streets were filled with strange folks of all kinds, the drunk, the cruel, the poor, and the unfortunate. Some of them seemed not to really care about Leonardo passing through, as if they were accustomed to seeing creatures and strangers all the time. Passing through the small village and into the nearby woods, Leonardo found himself at an isolated farm, yards away from the carriage that brought him there. The farm was acres of land, with cows, chickens, and other animals. Leonardo began to feel the burn for blood rise within his body. His predator instincts began to take over; his eyes turned to lust for his prey, and his fangs were ready to sink into the warmth of their blood. Leonardo knew that killing the animals was the only way he could survive without putting innocent blood on his hands. He consumed the blood of each animal, and with each taste, his strength returned, but only partial strength. He knew that the blood of the animals would only make his hunger subside. His body was at ease once again, but dawn was breaking soon, and Leonardo had to find a place to hide from the coming sunlight. Disregarding the blood that covered his clothes, Leonardo stepped out of the barn in search for a dark place to sleep. He looked over the vast land and found a toolshed next to the farmhouse; within seconds, he was inside the shed where he discovered a hidden cellar beneath the laid-out hay. It was an uncomfortable and empty place for one to hide from the dangers of the outside world, but it fit Leonardo's needs to escape from the deadly sun.

Daybreak came, and the farm owner could sense that something was not right with his farm. He decided to head over to the barn to check on the animals. Opening the doors, the farmer held his stomach in disgust, and the color from his complexion faded; there was blood everywhere. All the animals had been slaughtered and drained of their blood, leaving the stench of decomposing bodies in the air. With his heart racing, he was trying to grasp what he was seeing. *Father have mercy on my soul*, the farm owner said to himself. He decided that the best thing to do for him and his family was to leave and protect them from the beast that had destroyed his life's work. After reporting the occurrence to the village authorities, he and his family grabbed their valuables and left town because they had heard stories of past incidents of attacks within the town. Although the authorities later came and investigated, they could only conclude that it may have been a pack of wolves that came in the middle of the night and slaughtered the farm animals. There was simply no other evidence that could prove otherwise, but to some of the men, the air was filled with fear. A few of them had ideas about what could have been responsible for such a massacre. Yet none of them dared to speak or inform their captain.

The day passed, and Leonardo felt refreshed to see what the new night would bring, surviving on his own as a newborn. He came out of the cellar and still felt satisfied from the animal blood he drank the night before; however, he could not stay at the farm for long before the other vampires or the village authorities would find him. Coming out of the toolshed, Leonardo was cautious, making sure no one was around to see him. Aware that the unpleasant smell of dead carcasses still lingered in the air and that he looked like a vicious monster with blood on his clothes and hands, he headed to the house to clean himself up. Entering the house, Leonardo could sense that the owners had recently vacated the premises; picture frames were taken from the shelves, the chimney still had warm cinders burning, cabinets and drawers were left opened, and the aroma of a home-cooked meal was still within the house. For a brief moment, a flash of memories came across Leonardo's mind of his mother and sister baking and cooking dinner, a time that seemed a lifetime ago. Pushing those memories back in his mind, Leonardo headed for the bedroom to clean himself up and to find less conspicuous clothing. He walked through the narrow hallway and up the stairway, entering the main bedroom of the owner and his wife. More drawers had been left opened, with very few clothes left behind. He rummaged through what he could find and found an old suit close enough to his size, an outfit that would easily blend in with the townsfolk. As he was washing the blood off his face and hands in the water basin nearby, Leonardo began to think of what he had done; he still was not sure what would become of him after leaving Romulus's castle. Leonardo could still hear Romulus's words lingering in his mind. *There is much to be gained if you decide to leave your maker, Leonardo. You have a gift that could benefit this covenant, and I'd rather you stay and learn.* In order to keep moving forward, Leonardo decided to burn the evidence of his stained clothes, leave the farm, and see what this small village had to offer.

While being vigilant of his surroundings, Leonardo kept his head down, minding his own business among the evening crowd enjoying a late nightcap. Even though he was able to hear their thoughts, Leonardo did not care, nor was he bothered by the fear some of the people had as he walked past them. Shop after shop and house after house, Leonardo found himself learning that this town was the smallest town in Pennsylvania and was cared for by one generation to another. The village was filled with a small community of people that celebrated the little things; this was what gave the village life and something to look forward to in their mundane lives. Leonardo noted signs and decorations for a coming event, the fall harvest. Wreaths hung at every door, and patches of pumpkins sat at the top of their porches and by the dim lanterns that helped guide the path. Leonardo was able to see an open tavern from afar. The smell of alcohol and cigars surrounded the high-priced tavern, which was called Le Paradis de L'enfer. Through the tavern's French doors, he walked into a lavish lounge, occupied by high-class businessmen who were busy gambling with their money and who were draped with woman who would satisfy their intimate needs. Having already the attention from a few young prostitutes, Leonardo dismissed them and headed toward an open spot at the end of the bar where he could keep a watchful eye on the crowd. Hearing their deep secrets and temptations, he realized why most of them were at the tavern tonight: to gain money, to gamble away their fortune, to enjoy the intimacy of lust and fulfill their sexual desires, or to bury their sorrows in lethal liquid. He was saddened, knowing the shameful truth of what they all had become in this world. Even the aroma of the unfaithful lingered the tavern. Married man, seeking only the company and pleasure of other women in secrecy.

"Look who we have here, Lexa," a well-rounded woman by the name of Sheryl said as she came from satisfying one of her clients. She sat down at the nearest table and slugged the half-empty drink that someone had left behind. Sheryl was known in the tavern for her compelling attitude; she pleased many and knew how to handle her business. Coming from a low-class family that abandoned her years ago, she knew that working at the tavern was the only way she could support herself and her younger sister.

"Who?" Lexa asked, looking around to see who was in the tavern. She sat down next to Sheryl and was then able to see whom she was talking about. "Do you mean the man sitting at the far end of the bar?"

"Yes. I've never seen him here before, and he looks so delightful to taste," she said, slugging another drink from the next table over.

"Oh yes, and he truly is a pleasure to look at. But I don't know, Sheryl. There is something strange about him."

"Well then, just step aside, and I will show you how a real woman makes a man crawl on his knees." Sheryl said, fixing strands of her hair and reapplied her dark red lipstick.

As soon as Sheryl was about to approach the bar to make her move, another woman who worked in the tavern came and stood next to Leonardo and asked him for a drink. He politely ordered her a drink and tried to dismiss her, but she was persistent, and instead of walking away, she sat down next to him, wanting to get to know this mysterious man who was sitting alone at the bar. Sheryl was upset, realizing that she should have made her move sooner. She took a filled glass of hard liquor from the waitress passing by, drank it, and placed the glass back on the tray, knowing well enough that it was going to come out of her pay. She sat back down at the table with Lexa, worried that she and her sister were going to come up short on rent this month.

Sitting alongside Lexa, Sheryl had felt insulted that a beautiful man desired such an obsessive woman. She wanted to know who this stranger was that carried himself with such beauty and elegance. Jealousy waved over her like a dark cloud; she felt that two women beat her at her own game. She contemplated that the other woman had to possess some kind of unique charm about her that she would never have.

"Alydia, there is a gentleman asking for you at the casino table," a waitress said as she picked up the empty glasses from their table.

"Thank you."

"Lexa, stop telling people your real name. Remember what your name is. It's the only name that you will give out to people here. You are not Alydia anymore," Sheryl explained.

Lexa apologized to Sheryl and obeying what she was told, she headed to the casino table to entertain the gentleman who asked for her.

Seated at the end of the bar, Leonardo was trying not to look out of place by talking to the young woman. Her name was Flora, and she was trying hard to seduce him, but she was failing greatly. He had no interest in her but was playing along to ease the onlookers around the bar. She invaded his personal space, as her leg was touching his, her hand was on his thigh, and she was asking many questions, "I've never seen you here before. Are you new in these parts? Where are you from? What brings you into town?" Flora asked. He gave very vague answers. As Leonardo turned to acknowledge Flora, he caught sight of two women looking at him from across the room. Sheryl gave a slight nod to greet him, while Lexa turned away out of shyness.

Following what was catching Leonardo's eye, Flora realized that he was glancing at the other girls. She grabbed his hand and, before he could stop her, brought him to the crowded dance floor that was filled with drunken men dancing with women eager for their money. With graciousness, Leonardo led the way. As they danced and Leonardo blended in with the crowd, he felt in control, and for a moment he felt free that he was on his own. It was the same atmosphere he had felt when he was a young boy; it was this state of mind that made him forget the fierce monster he was. Unexpectedly, Flora wrapped her arm around his neck and brought herself to his lips. "You have such tasteful lips," She said. Leonardo was taken aback and gracefully pushed her away, but she didn't let down. She pulled him away from the crowd and asked Leonardo, "Do you wish to go somewhere private, my love?" Flora asked. Admiring her strong will and determined personality, he agreed to entertain her. "Lead the way," Leonard replied. As they were heading out, Leonardo took another glance at Sheryl and Lexa sitting at the casino table and was taken aback by the blushing woman sitting there. Lexa was a petite young girl of average height with dark brown hair pinned up to showcase her features, but what mesmerized Leonardo were her familiar round eyes. It was as if he knew who she was, but he couldn't pinpoint the memory of her.

Again, Leonardo was brought back to Flora's attention when they reached the back alley of the tavern. She pushed him against the brick wall and desperately began to kiss him as she pushed herself against his sturdy body. "Make me yours," Flora said. Instead of pushing her away, he relaxed for an instant, remembering that he was alone on his own now. "Take me, my love," She demanded. His hands moved with her body, embracing her sexual desires, and as his lips moved with hers, he took control and moved her against the wall. Leonardo began to feel his instincts grow in unexpected places. Without warning, memories of the blood he had shed with Boris came to mind, and it was now too late to dismiss the burning thirst of blood that had blossomed. Her warmth began to satisfy his cold, dead body, and in the act of Flora unbuttoning his dress coat and shirt, Leonardo made his way down to her bare neck, as she moaned in pleasure. Without thinking twice about his actions, Leonardo sunk his fangs into her. With the amount of alcohol, she had consumed, she felt little pain as her blood ran through his body, subsiding the fire that burned under his skin and dismissing his dark thoughts. At the edge of his satisfaction, Leonardo immediately came back to his senses and was shocked at the bloody woman in his arms. Looking at the bite marks he left on her neck and the blood that was spilt all over her clothes, he could still hear her breathing and believed that she still had a chance to live. "What have I done?" Leonardo said, in barely a whisper. He picked her up in his arms and in a flash of light arrived at the steps of the town's physician, but a second after they arrived, it was too late for Flora's life to be saved. As Leonardo heard the last rhythm of her heartbeat fade away, he realized the full consequences. He swiftly left the scene, leaving Flora to rest in peace.

All Leonardo wanted to do was escape this world and end his life, no matter what the cost.

I deserve to suffer, Leonardo thought. He was never a killer, but now because of Boris's selfishness and influence, he had become one.

Leonardo walked for miles, having an internal struggle on whether to walk to the ends of the earth until the sun rose or to keep fighting to use this new life to find his sister and get the truth about his family's death. In the end, he knew that he had to make a life-or-death decision.

Miles later, as he was walking down the deserted road, he pulled out a handkerchief from his breast pocket and started to clean Flora's blood from his hands and from around his mouth as best he could. Occupied by his thoughts and the blood that stained him, Leonardo was unaware of the direction he was heading when he came across an old abandoned church. The church was named after the saint of hope, St. Jude Thaddeus Catholic Church. From his mother's teachings, he remembered that St. Jude Thaddeus was a disciple that urged others not to give up and to keep on fighting.

"After all that has happened and all that I have suffered, is this a sign to keep fighting?" Leonardo asked the empty black sky.

The church seemed to have been built during the sixteenth century. It was an average-sized building with cracked walls and faded paint. Uncertain if he was no longer worthy to even go in, he knew he had to do what he must to stay hidden. Entering the crumbling building, he stepped inside the church and was dazed by the protective angel hovering over the entryway. Everything around the angel was almost in ruins, but the angel remained intact. He wandered around to see the history and spirit that this place once held and to find an area that was dark enough to rest before the sun rose again. As it seemed that his thoughts were answered, he walked over to the back of the church and to his satisfaction came across an empty, windowless room filled with various sized coffins. Leonardo decided that the church would be a safe place to stay for the time being, and he could survive off the rats and the animals that lurked around. From the long night, Leonardo knew that he needed to keep fighting; he wasn't going to give up on his lost family, and most of all, he wasn't going to give up on his sister; the only true family he might have left in this dark and cruel world. He dusted off one of the larger coffins, gracefully got inside, and closed it. For a moment, awake in the darkness, Leonardo vowed to himself that he would not take another human life, and he hoped that tomorrow's moonlight would bring a better life of solidarity. *This is not the end,* He thought, as he closed his eyes and fell into a deep state of stillness.

X

Winter 1789

The sun rose day after day, and the moon glistened in the dark sky night after night. Time had passed since the night Leonardo took his vow. He had been feeding on animals, mainly rats that lingered around the old church. Some days he was lucky enough to feed off on deer in the nearby woods, or a lone bear that was hunting for food. Throughout the nights, Leonardo kept to himself, using this time, with his limited strength, to learn how to control the darkness that resided within him.

The church was gradually coming back to life, as Leonardo had been trying to make it the way it once was. With the crumbling stones and bricks that he moved to a pile outside to clear the walkway of the aisle, and with the hanging lights dusted off, the moonlight was able to come through the old stained-glass windows and shine upon the only standing crucifix in the room. Admiring the half-broken crucifix that hung high at the end of the church, Leonardo wondered if there was really a God out there. It seemed that his prayers were never answered; he gave and gave and received nothing in return, only this life that Boris gave him.

"If you are really there, why did you leave me to live alone? Why did you destine for me to become the devil's servant and to kill your children for my own satisfaction and survival?" Leonardo cried out loud.

Studying every carved line of the man suspended on the cross, Jesus Christ, with his head bowed down, Leonardo pondered for a moment. After everything he had done in his life, would he ever meet Jesus, who, according to scripture, *died for our sins?* Leonardo began to feel a sense of light inside of him; it seemed he found the way to his answers. It was an overwhelming feeling but a virtuous feeling nevertheless. He knew what he had to do to find the truth, and to do so, he had to stop hiding behind the shadows and leave the church. He knew that if he stayed, this new life would be wasted.

With a new purpose, it seemed that the world knew what was coming; it had started to rain. There was a storm headed his way, so Leonardo decided to head out to his journey the next night. He closed up all the windows and all the doors, but as he was heading to close the main door of the entrance to the church, a man appeared drenched from the rain, "Sir, please, I beg that I could stay inside this church for just the night. I have no home to go to, I promise that I will leave first thing in the morning," The man said. Leonardo knew well enough that he couldn't let the man stay, because of the danger the man would be in by staying under the same roof with a vampire. Yet he felt sorry for the man, for he remembered how it felt to be traveling without shelter. Leonardo took the risk and let the man stay in the church. "You may stay, but only for tonight."

With appreciation, the man thanked Leonardo and started to relax. The man was amazed at the architecture of the old church, as Leonardo had been when he first took shelter there. With no introduction, the man was carefree and dismissive of the way Leonardo looked as Leonardo made his way around, catching the raindrops coming through the broken roof, wearing his overused suit and dirty dress shoes.

"Have you stayed here long?" the man asked, as if he already knew the answer.

Speculating on how much information Leonardo wanted to give, he told him that he had stayed at the church for only a short period of time.

"But I will be leaving once the storm passes," Leonardo continued to explain.

"Is this your church?" the man said trying to make conversation.

"No."

"I see."

The man began to settle himself with his belongings in one of the back pews. Meanwhile, Leonardo put the last pail near the altar, as now the church sung a symphony of steady raindrops. After seeing that the man was settling in to sleep for the night, Leonardo made his way to the back room where his coffin was. Suddenly, an aroma that Leonardo hadn't tasted in years filled the air. "I know this smell," He said to himself. Leonardo was suffocating within the walls of the church, and everything was closing in on him. He turned around and saw that the man had accidentally slit his hand with his hunting knife; not paying any attention to how it happened, blood was trickling out from a cut on his lower palm. Leonardo was becoming high from the familiar yet distant smell of warm human blood. As if someone else took control of his body, in a flash of light Leonardo took the man by the neck and absorbed every ounce of blood until the man's heartbeat began to fade.

The darkness that was silent for so long now rose within Leonardo. He felt his full strength again, but this time he realized that he was at his fullest potential. With his regained strength, he had now become what he had denied himself to be, and with these powers, he could live as a true vampire without fear, morals, or persecution. Leonardo felt a more powerful grip within his hands, and his eyesight was sharper than ever. His strength and speed had drastically increased, and his senses rose up. It was a sensational feeling that he couldn't fully describe, but he knew he should embrace his powers. *Yes, finally it is time,* He thought. Looking down at the lifeless body at his feet, Leonardo knew that the first thing he had to do was to get rid of the body. However, before doing so, Leonardo rummaged through the man's belongings to find enough money to buy new clothes. Grabbing the man's body, as if he weighed the amount of a feather, and the rest of his belongings, Leonardo went outside in the heavy storm and headed toward the swallowing grounds of the cemetery. Picking up a rusty shovel, Leonardo began to dig a grave for the man. Rapidly he dug up six feet of dirt and put the dead corpse in, and then he started to shovel the dirt back in. Before tossing the dead man's belongings into the grave, Leonardo got hold of a matchbox from his sack, thinking of a good use for it. Satisfied by his thorough completion, Leonardo went back in the church, and without any remorse for what he had done, he slept restfully in his coffin until sunset.

By the next night, Leonardo felt more alive than ever. He was no longer weak, nor did he feel that he had to hide from the world any longer. Moving on from the embodiment of his weakness, Leonardo took the matchbox, that he had taken from the man who was now buried six feet in the ground and lit what was his home for one year on fire. From a distance, he stood by and watched as the old church burned and crumbled to the ground. "And so, it begins," He said to himself. Amused by how little effort it took to change from someone so powerless to a vampire that could kill on a rampage, Leonardo thought it was time to head back to Romulus's castle, yet not before changing into a proper man. With his stolen money, Leonardo went into the village and bought a new suit. With his newfound confidence and grown ego, he turned himself into an elegant and suitable man of power; he dressed in a dark blue suit sewn in gold threading and accompanied by a top hat and silver engraved staff. Leonardo felt like a changed man, and he enjoyed every moment of it.

Walking through the unchanging town, Leonardo was a different person from when first he walked through a year ago. People passing acknowledged him as someone with importance and wealth, rather than someone who was afraid and weak. As he walked through the village, women of all ages stared at him, and some even giggled amongst themselves, seeing such a handsome man. It seemed that Leonardo was being seen as a rich and powerful man who could get anything he wanted. However, all Leonardo cared about was how good this all felt to him—the beauty, the power, and most of all, the ability to do whatever he desired at any given moment. Turning the corner, Leonardo caught sight of the tavern and decided to make a visit where he had once enjoyed the company of Flora.

It was as if nothing had been touched since his last visit, nor had people's thoughts changed over the years, as Leonardo entered the tavern and began to hear everyone's deep thoughts. Embracing the fumes of liquor and cigars, Leonardo made his way to the gambling table. Knowing that he could use his subconscious ability to win, he decided to use the remaining money he had and turn it into more money that he could use for his journey ahead. Sitting down at the table, he greeted the four other men about to start a new game. With some hesitation from the other men, due to the fact that they didn't know Leonardo, nor had they seen his face around the tavern before, Leonardo was welcomed to place a bet and start the game.

Working her way around the tavern, Sheryl was talking to one of her returning clients when she noticed Leonardo's familiar stature. She was glad to see him again and eager to be able to get her chance with him after all this time; she excused herself and gladly approached Leonardo. Coming up from behind him at the gambling table, she brushed her hand along his shoulders and greeted all the gentlemen seated at the table, and then she finally greeted Leonardo.

"Hello, sir. I'm so glad to see you here again," Sheryl said with a growing smile.

"It's my pleasure," Leonardo replied as he turned and kissed her hand that was resting on his shoulder.

Every bone in her body desired him, and she was hoping that for at least one night she could spend the night with him.

"May I ask, what kept you from the tavern for so long? Surely, a powerful and handsome man like you would enjoy the company of an experienced woman."

"Let's just say that I was out of town for some time."

"Well, in that case, might I give you a proper welcome back?" Sheryl said, rubbing seductively against his forearm.

Leonardo looked toward the bar and the rest of the tavern and asked where the woman he saw last time was.

"You mean Flora?" Sheryl asked, trying to cover her jealously. "My love, you shouldn't be concerned about her. Believe me when I say that no one cares what happens around here; theft, lies, and murders—it is all part of the village. Everyone minds their own business in these parts."

"Actually, my dear, I meant your other friend."

"Oh, you mean Lexa," Sheryl responded curiously as she removed her hand from his arm and slowly pulled away, feeling disappointed yet again.

"Yes, Lexa."

"She is not here anymore. About a year ago, Lexa and some of her former slave friends decided to go back to their hometown of Pittsburgh."

"Pittsburgh, you say?" Leonardo said.

"Thinking of paying a visit to a worthless girl? What is she to you? I can't imagine you liking her, sir." Sheryl tried her best to hide her jealousy.

"Don't you worry your pretty little head about that, but let's just say that she strikes my interest," Leonardo replied.

"Thank you, gentlemen, for your time. It has been a great pleasure." With another win, Leonardo picked up his winnings, his staff, and his hat and excused himself from the gambling table. "Excuse me, Madam Sheryl, thank you for your company, but I must leave now. Next time I plan a visit to Le Paradis de L'enfer, hopefully then may I intrigue you with a nightcap."

Ready to head out of the tavern, Leonardo thought that maybe he should be generous toward Sheryl before leaving on his journey. He turned around, grabbed her by the waist, pulled her in, and gave her a hard kiss on the lips. Leonardo pulled away, leaving Sheryl standing breathless and stunned by what just happened.

"Until next time," Leonardo said with a sinister smirk forming across his face.

Feeling pleased with himself, Leonardo headed out to pay a visit to some old friends.

✲　✲　✲　✲

Back along the outskirts of Pittsburgh, Alydia, Simon, and their new-found friend, Michael, were living together to make ends meet. The house belonged to Michael's grandparents before they passed it along to him. He had offered it to Alydia and Simon in exchange for company and good food. The house was two stories and surrounded by a decent amount of land.

Meanwhile, Alydia was sitting down near a window looking out at the beauty of the full moon. She was filled with great sadness, as she was thinking of the past and was reminded of better times. Unexpectedly, Simon entered into the room interrupted her thoughts and sitting next to her, trying to give her the comfort and reassurance she needed.

"Please, you must get some rest, Alydia. You can't keep feeling guilty for the past; it wasn't your fault," Simon pleaded; feeling pity for her, as he knew what she was going through.

"It's not that easy, Simon. I have that nightmare every night, and it consumes my thoughts every day," Alydia explained.

"I know what you are going through. I lost both my brother and my mother that day too. Nonetheless, you and I both know that life must go on."

"I know," Alydia replied with tears in her eyes.

"Where is Michael?" Simon asked.

"He is asleep. He went to bed about an hour ago, after supper," Alydia said, while taking composure of herself before the tears could fall.

"You must get some sleep too, Alydia. We have another long day of work ahead of us."

Alydia knew that Simon was right, but she didn't want to have another nightmare about her family. She continued to watch the moon, dwelling on what could have been and what should be done.

Knowing that Alydia was stubborn, Simon begged her again to get some sleep, and as if coming out of a daze, Alydia obeyed and headed to her room for another sleepless night.

XI

Finally making his way to Romulus's castle, Leonardo was ready to face the adversaries he had run away from. Now as a stronger and fiercer vampire, he was prepared to do what was necessary to anyone that might stand in his way and question him. However, coming upon the entrance, he knew that something had changed since his last visit. Leonardo got off the stolen horse he took from the tavern and tied him against the railings of the gate. Walking past the gates that protected the castle grounds, he came near the front door and to his surprise found that it was left open. Cautiously opening the door, Leonardo could see that the castle had been abandoned for quite some time; rats and spiders seemed to nest in the emptiness that echoed throughout the walls. *What is the meaning of this?* He thought. Leonardo could hear no voices or sense any other vampire around. He began walking the hallways where he once roamed, looking for any signs of why they all decided to leave. Even the rooms that horrified him were left empty. He began to run toward the dungeon where he had met the record keeper, Atticus, and found nothing. "Atticus!" Leonardo called out. Then he decided to run to the high tower, and once he got there, everything was gone. All of the records, books, articles, and the old paintings were gone from the shelves. Suddenly he spotted a handwritten letter on the floor:

The darkest hours of the Vampyr has finally come forth. You shall not escape the wrath of the one who shall bring chaos and despair to the covenants. This prophecy of the immortals looks down upon the descendants of the old king, who will come forth with new blood to cease all and create a new rule. Thus, will rain fire and destruction upon all. He shall become lord and master, who will seek total darkness through this new order. A new dawn has arrived, where none will be able to escape. The one to fulfill this prophecy is alive and coming!

Angry and confused, Leonardo yelled out and began to smash the shelves together, making them collapse throughout the room. It seemed that one of the ancient prophecies foretelling the coming of a vampire lord was coming true. It didn't matter to Leonardo; the only thought that ran through his mind was to find the one who caused all this madness. "Cowards! You are all cowards!" Leonardo yelled out in anger. Feeling outraged at the thought that he couldn't show his full potential to his maker and to those who questioned his will of being a vampire, he grabbed an iron candelabrum that was standing nearby, snapped it in half, and threw it across the room. He was disappointed that he wasn't able to prove himself to them and show that he was worthy enough to be one of them. He walked through the dark hallways and arrived at the terrace where he once spoke to Romulus and Ilene. He stood watching over the vast land that was covered in darkness, remembering how he was seen as a fool and a puppet within the covenant. Feeling the cold breeze, he began to feel at ease once more. The moonlight gleamed down upon him, making him feel powerful and in control again. He frowned as he looked down from the terrace, feeling disappointed in the covenant. He knew that he had to continue on. He jumped off from the terrace and landed on the ground, producing a crater into the cement ground. Turning his back on the castle one last time, Leonardo cursed them as they should be damned to hell.

* * * *

Outside the castle, just beyond the nearby woods, an enigmatic red-cloaked female figure stood watch as Leonardo rushed out of the castle. Observing what had occurred from a distance, she was compelled to notice that everything was coming along the way it had been planned. Satisfied, she turned around and walked back into the darkness of the forest.

* * * *

Getting back on his horse again, Leonardo galloped through the forest, heading toward Pittsburgh. He speculated on what could have happened to everyone who had resided in the castle. Did they leave? Or had they been murdered in some unknown way? Either way, he felt satisfied that they were no longer there. Now he didn't have to feel dominated by his master or any other vampire.

Another day of light was forthcoming, and he wouldn't be able to reach Pittsburgh in time. His surroundings became familiar as he realized where he was. He knew that a few miles away, the cave where he and Boris escaped to, after not taking the life he was told to take at the Williams' banquet, was the safest place to take cover from the approaching daylight. Leonardo dismounted his horse and headed inside the cave, pulling the horse inside with him. They went deep inside the cave, exactly where he once rested. Recalling that at that time he hadn't accepted his abilities, Leonardo looked up to the ceiling of the cave and smiled. Securing the horse from fleeing, he began his way towards the side of the cave, mimicking Boris's footsteps. As if he knew how to do it all this time, he stretched one foot in front of the other and began climbing along the wall. He could feel an overwhelming power flowing through him that prevented him from falling. "Not incompetent anymore, now am I?". Leonardo could feel the rocks making contact with his hands and feet, and it felt as if there was no sense of gravity to hold him down. Certainly, the laws of physics where being blown away by the incredible gifts that the vampire possessed. Never in his lifetime as a mortal could he have guessed how different he would become from the rest of the world. Now he stood where Boris was once suspended over him. He was hanging upside down like a bat prepared to take his prey. He began to laugh, as his ominous voice echoed within the sanctified cave; Leonardo felt such bliss and took pride in finally being able to reach his true abilities, proving that he wasn't a disappointment anymore. Satisfied with himself, Leonardo crossed his arms around his chest and began to fall asleep in preparation for a new night of blood, pleasure, and mischief.

*   *   *   *

Awake for a new day, Alydia, Simon, and Michael were preparing for a full day of doing chores and making ends meet by working at the local market. Alydia had a moment of reflection, giving out a small prayer that the day would be fruitful. "Oh, Heavenly Father, I pray that this day may be filled with your love and grace. Give us the strength, and courage oh Lord to keep on going forward. Shield me from any evil, and temptations. Forgive me for my sins, and past wrong doings against thy will. Have mercy on my soul, oh Heavenly Father. I ask this in the name of our Lord, and savior, Jesus Christ. Amen" Satisfied with her prayer, she began her day.

Putting on her clothes, combing her hair gently, and thinking about the endless possibilities that could present themselves, she remembered when her mother used to help her get ready for the day when she was little. Her little brother, Leonardo, was always making jokes about how she was always treated like a doll by their mother. Simon, in the other room, was in deep thought as he stood by the window in silence. Thinking about the journey ahead with Alydia, he also remembered his own brother and mother when they were still alive. He would not admit it, but he really missed them. He knew he had to be strong for Alydia and not be a burden to her. He shook off his feelings and continued getting dressed and prepared for the day.

Alydia made her way down the stairs and into the kitchen and started cooking breakfast for them. It wouldn't take long for Simon to come down to help her set up the food before Michael arrived to eat with them. When they were all gathered at the table to eat breakfast, there was a moment of silence before Alydia said, "I cannot explain why, but I feel that there is something different in the air today."

"Something bad or something good?" Simon asked.

"I am not sure yet, but I can sense something is going to happen."

"What do you mean?" Simon asked, a worried look on his face.

"I don't know what, or how, or even when, but I can just sense that something is coming."

"Your mind is probably playing tricks on you, darling, due to the fact that you haven't gotten a good night's rest in a while. You shouldn't worry so much," Michael said, taking bites of his buttered bread.

"Maybe you are right, Michael," Alydia said while staring down at her loaf of bread in deep thought.

"We have all been through our fair share of hardships, but nothing will happen, Alydia. We need to keep on moving forward in order to go on with our lives," Michael went on to say.

Feeling a little less troubled, Alydia nodded in agreement. After finishing her breakfast, she went on her way to start the chores around the house as Michael and Simon headed out to work at the market.

Meanwhile, trying to keep everything in control, Simon knew that Alydia was right. He too felt something stirring in the air, but he did not want to make Alydia or Michael more worried, so he kept his feelings to himself and carried on to another workday.

The day went on as Michael and Simon worked their way to earn enough to get by. While Alydia was caring for the only land they had, she tried to occupy herself enough to not worry about what might lie ahead in this strange new air. So, every day like clockwork, she recollected the memories she had of her family. Hanging up the laundered clothes on the clothesline, she remembered helping her mother as a young girl. What Alydia missed the most was how Leonardo would come running through the clothes with his arms flapping up and down like a bird, until her father would come and make Leonardo behave. No matter how hard she tried, her nightmares would always prevail over the good memories she had.

"Alydia! Take Simon with you and get out of here! Do it, now!" Marco yelled out. As she grabbed Simon from his hand, she looked back and could see a tall ghostly figure ready to attack Marco. "Father!" She yelled in fear. "Run!" he screamed. Running away with Simon as fast as they could, realizing that they might never see them alive again. There was nothing she could do.

These memories were now engraved in her mind. Yet, like clockwork again, the memories were dismissed with the realization of what reality was for her now. Her whole family was dead and gone, and she had nothing to remember them by other than the blood that ran through her veins. Alydia had often wondered about what came upon the house she and her family once lived in, and she often fantasized that her family was still alive somewhere. Unfortunately, she knew that it was impossible; stories spread quickly around Pittsburgh, and everyone concluded that wolves had slaughtered the Le' Muerte family that night. With a heavy sigh in trying to accept that she was possibly the only Le' Muerte alive, Alydia took the empty laundry basket and headed inside to start on dinner.

Alydia, Simon, and Michael didn't have much. Then again, like her mother, Alydia knew how to make something extraordinary out of very little. With the few vegetables she grew and the meat Michael was able to bargain for in the market, Alydia was able to make a stew for dinner, accompanied by the last loaf of bread they had for the month. By the time Alydia had finished making dinner, Michael and Simon had made their way back from work, and they were all now sitting around the table, contemplating the day that had gone by.

"I've heard word from my cousins up north of Pittsburgh that they need help with their farmland or they will lose everything they've worked for," Michael said.

"I'm so sorry to hear that, Michael. What are you going to do? Move up north?" Simon asked.

"Well, yes. I can't leave my family behind. I will take what I've earned from working at the market and do what I can to help them," Michael explained. "Why don't you both come with me? We can't keep living on one decent meal a month, based on the pay that we are getting here. Besides, there is more work and better pay up north."

"We have made it just fine so far," Alydia said, stopping Michael to speak any further.

"Yes, we have, Alydia, but to what expense? If there is a chance for us to live better lives without having to worry about affording enough food for the next month or being treated poorly when we have nothing to offer to our community, then we should take it," Michael explained.

Alydia could see that Michael had given this much thought. Michael went on to explain how they had saved up enough money to do the two-day trip up north toward Buffalo Swamp to the town of Wyoming, with some extra money left over for provisions. Michael even suggested selling the cottage they currently had, to be able to get a new and probably better cottage where they were heading. However, Alydia knew that this was a mistake. She couldn't just pick up her things and leave, knowing that her brother might return home someday or at least try to find the truth behind the answers she was seeking about her family's death. Pittsburgh was her home, and she wasn't ready to leave it all behind to start a new life somewhere else, even if it meant having a better lifestyle or not worrying about food or being treated poorly.

"No!" Alydia said, interrupting Michael's continuing persuasion of moving.

Michael looked at her with confusion as Alydia was planning on what she was going to say next.

"I mean ... I can't. I can't just pick up everything and leave the chance of finding Leonardo, or at least the truth of what happened to my family."

"Alydia, it has been sixteen years. You can't keep doing this to yourself. You can't keep blaming yourself for your family's death," Simon stated. "I know what you are going through. I was there that night too. Remember?"

"That's the thing, Simon. I remember everything from that night, as if it happened yesterday. I remember the screaming, the blood, and the terrible noise of the monster that still rings in my ears at night as I fail to get an ounce of sleep."

Simon stared at Alydia, as the memories were vivid in his mind as well. Michael, on the other hand, just stood there, dumbfounded, for this was the first time he heard what happened to their families in detail.

"Simon, I have this deep feeling that my brother is still out there. You would hesitate to leave too if you knew, by some chance, that David was still alive out there," Alydia said, without holding back her emotions.

Simon didn't know what to say. He knew she was right, but he also knew that life went on. Before he could respond, Michael said that he would stay behind to support her and help find her brother, if by some chance he was still out there.

"I can't let you do that. Your family needs you more," Alydia said. "I appreciate all that we have done together here, but I believe that the best thing for you to do is to move north, and we will stay behind. I will return to my own land eventually; perhaps I may find something there. Simon, you are more than welcome to leave with him if you choose to."

"I can't let you do that. I promised I would keep you safe, so I am staying with you, and that is not up for discussion, Alydia," Simon said.

Even though Michael was dissatisfied with the idea that Alydia and Simon were going to be left behind, he agreed to the plan. "Alright, do as you please," Michael said. He knew that this was the only way to please everyone and to give her one last opportunity to realize that Leonardo was gone, like everyone else.

Within the next two days, Michael prepared what he needed and began his journey up north. Alydia and Simon were left behind to pursue their own journey back to the place where it all began.

XII

The darkness of the night had fallen upon the town when Leonardo woke up, realizing that someone else was in the cave with him, as he could sense a familiar scent that he was once drawn to. He abruptly dropped down to the floor of the cave and with ease stood up to be inches away from the unwelcomed guest.

"Hello again," she said with her voice resonating throughout the cave.

"Now, this is a surprise, Ilene," Leonardo said.

"This is the last place I thought I would find you. But it wasn't too hard to find you, as it would be just as easy for any other vampire to get to you."

"Well, the last person I expected to come looking for me was you," Leonardo replied, giving her no acknowledgment of joy from her presence.

Distracted by Leonardo's new sense of preservation and confidence, Ilene sensed that he actually wanted to be found.

"You seem different, Leonardo. It is as if you have found a new sense of preservation as a vampire."

"Yes, I have. Thank you for taking notice. I believe that it was time for me to rise up and become the newborn that I am meant to be."

Taking one step toward Leonardo and taking a hold of his hands, Ilene looked within his eyes and tried to find any sign of humanity still left in him.

"Come away with me, Leonardo, I beg you. Let me show you a new world as I told you a year ago, back at Romulus's castle."

"You really think you can save me from all this?" Leonardo asked, wondering what better world she could be talking about. Nothing could be better than the world he was living in now.

"Yes, I can. I promised you I would take both of us away from all this madness," Ilene replied in a desperate tone, as if she was ready to leave in any moment.

Leonardo took a brief moment to think about what Ilene was offering. Feeling her hands on his hands and looking fiercely into her eyes, he knew that deep within there was a chance for him to truly escape all this. However, the part of him that enjoyed the blood and pleasure of this new life was much stronger.

"If it was at any other moment before this, I would have accepted your offer. Sorry to disappoint you, but you are too late. I am not that scared little boy anymore, and I am not going back to that. I am not leaving who I truly am and what this world has to offer me."

Leonardo pulled his hands from Ilene's grasp and stepped back, turning his back on her.

"What are you saying?" Ilene asked.

"I am not running away anymore, Ilene!" Leonardo exclaimed, snapping back toward her. "I will not be used as an unworthy vampire as I was before. I see with new eyes, and I now understand the meaning of this life, and with that, I will accept my fate of being what I was created to be."

With a sinister look, Leonardo grabbed Ilene in a dance and began to move around the cave as if he was imagining them at a grand ball. "I actually have a new proposal for you. What if you gave into your vampire instincts, as I have, and then we can run away together? Imagine it, Ilene. We can rule the Vampyr world, and we would do it together, side by side."

"No, you cannot be telling me this. This is not you, Leonardo!" Ilene cried out, forcing their dance to stop midway in a turn as she pushed Leonardo away.

"Oh, but it is, Ilene. This is the way of the Vampyr, and I must tell you that it feels so glorious to have this power. The peace you feel when drinking human blood as it runs through your body, the rush of satisfaction, and the pleasure of accepting what you are," Leonardo explained.

"You sound just like my maker," Ilene said in disbelief. "Boris finally made you into the vampire he always desired."

Leonardo took a moment to process what Ilene just admitted to him. He gave her a serious look and gradually took a few steps toward her. Noticing that she wasn't stepping back from him, he continued to move forward, lightly pressing his body against hers and gently pressing his hands upon her shoulders.

"Ilene, I would love to feel your beautiful lips and your delicate hands on me. If you come with me on this journey, then maybe I can show you the world that you are missing," Leonardo said while touching her jaw line.

Ilene turned her face away, moving away from where his hands were going. "I don't know who you are anymore. You are not the Leonardo I spoke to that night on the terrace."

"Exactly. I am better than who I was then."

"No, you are not! You have become exactly like all the others, careless and cold," Ilene said, using her strength to push Leonardo off and putting enough space between them by standing across the cave. "I cannot believe you. I was a fool to believe that you would be different. I was greatly mistaken."

Leonardo was getting upset at Ilene's refusal to join him. He didn't want to hear her opinions anymore, yet deep down within him, the part of him that he had yet to let go of could feel her pain and knew that it was too late to turn back.

"I know who you are, Ilene," He said.

"You don't know anything, Leonardo," Ilene replied with anger. "You think by having me by your side will bring salvation? Do you really think I would fill your void of emptiness? There is no road to salvation for you. Your maker didn't force you to kill your father, because you wanted to do it. Of all the disgusting creatures, you deserve to be what you are." Hesitating to look Leonardo directly in his eyes, she gave one last say in the matter. "This is your chance to be free from everything. You once told me that by living this life as a vampire, one would become a monster, and that is what you have become. My dear Leonardo, you are right. You have changed, but I will always remember the man that stood before me under the flickering fireplace and spoke of a better life. I just hope it is not too late to save that man."

Her words, barely an undertone and audible only to vampire ears, got under Leonardo's skin. At the moment that his thoughts became clear enough to explain to her that the man she remembered no longer existed, she vanished from his sight.

Despite the fact that Ilene's words triggered something inside of Leonardo, his instincts took over and erased his emotions. He knew that it was time to finish what he had come back to do. He headed out of the cave as he grabbed his belongings and went to his horse. On top of his horse, he adjusted his hat and waistcoat and went on his way toward Pittsburgh with one goal in mind.

All things considered, Leonardo knew that this time he would be able to challenge Boris and not be a failure; unlike the last time they fought.

Along the trail, Leonardo imagined his victory against Boris and the entire Dominus covenant that thought he was worthless. He wanted to be the king sitting on the high throne of his own castle. Suddenly, a flock of bats came swarming through the misty woods. Leonardo could sense that there was something strange lingering close by. He hastily turned the horse around and was surprised to find that no one was there. However, the howling of the wolves that appeared from the shadows quickly startled the horse. Three alpha wolves stood before him, each showing its sharp teeth and emitting a rising growl from inside. Both Leonardo and the wolves showed no fear but were threatened by each other as the wolves growled viciously in hunger. Leonardo knew that they were no threat to him. Calming his horse down, Leonardo stared into their eyes and gave a low, menacing growl until the wolves whimpered off in fright. "Magnificent creatures they are." He said. Taking pleasure in having frightened the wolves, Leonardo moved along his horse to continue his journey toward Pittsburgh.

☼   ☼   ☼   ☼

Within the darkness of the trail to Pittsburgh, where Leonardo was headed, the red-cloaked female figure continued her mission of completing her plan. Though her plan had almost ended when Leonardo briefly got sight of her, she thanked the heavens for bringing the wolves as a distraction. For now, she had to keep low, until the right opportunity presented itself in order for her to execute her plan.

☼   ☼   ☼   ☼

Finally, Leonardo was able to reach the town's lights that guided the townspeople toward the backdrop of mountains and continuous nightlife activity. It was exactly the same as it had been when he was bought by Mr. Cooper from the slave trade. Rows of houses and shops occupied the center of the town, and groups of people passed him by as Leonardo galloped his way down the street with a new sense of determination. It was all the same as he remembered. However, this time, the streets and neighboring rooftops were covered with a blanket of white snow, and children were playing outside as they enjoyed the welcoming season.

Getting down from his horse to walk the rest of the way, he was content with the fact that no one would remember him after being away for so long. Passing through the streets and the groups of people, Leonardo caught sight of a young boy making his way through by cautiously trying to grab and steal what he could get his hands on. Leonardo was reminded that once he too was living on the streets of Pittsburgh when he was a young boy. In a swift motion, Leonardo moved in front of the boy and pulled him away from the wallet he was about to steal. Standing now within the shadows of the nearest alleyway, the boy was about to argue and yell at the man who ruined his plan for a week's worth of food, but then the boy stood still in fright, facing the man standing in front of him. Worried that the boy might scream and run, Leonardo placed his long, thin finger over his lips as a gesture to stay quiet and to not be afraid. The young boy who seemed to be the age of twelve nervously looked in Leonardo's eyes, and with the little courage he had, he asked what he wanted from him.

"I did not pull you aside to acquire something from you, boy. You could at least express your gratitude for saving you from the dangers of becoming a slave," Leonardo stated.

"I wasn't in any danger, sir! Besides, I can take care of myself—have been doing so for the past couple of years," the boy exclaimed.

Leonardo smiled in amusement. Softly grabbing the boy by the shoulder, he turned him around to show him the opening view of the village.

"You see there," Leonardo said, acknowledging the two authorities who seemed to be searching for someone in the crowd. "They were about to arrest you for stealing the wallet you were about to take. If it wasn't for me, you would have been shipped off to the slave trade by morning."

The boy didn't let down his guard, but he knew that the man was right. With a hesitant tone, he thanked him and again asked him what he wanted from him.

"I have no more desire for this horse. He is yours now to keep," Leonardo said.

The young, frightened boy accepted his offer and took the horse from Leonardo's cold hands. Startled by Leonardo's long, sharp nails, the boy took a step back.

"Are you a monster?" the boy asked.

"Perhaps. That depends on you," Leonardo replied with a slight smile.

Not wanting to know more about the terrifying man standing in front of him, the boy took the horse and continued on his journey as quickly his legs could go. When the boy was just few feet away with the horse, Leonardo said, stopping the boy on his tracks, "One more thing. Stay away from a man by the name of Thomas Hill. He is the real monster you should be worried about." Leonardo chuckled under his breath, as he knew he had scared the young boy.

Leonardo stepped out of the alleyway, and just before he continued his way through the town, he caught sight of the young woman he recognized at Le Paradis de L'enfer.

Alexa, he thought. She was walking along the street with a young man next to her.

Is he her slave? Husband? or Lover?

Leonardo decided to follow her, hoping that she would be his next victim. He felt as if nothing else mattered but to get the girl to fall under his seduction. The ambition and the joy of feeling such pleasure of being in the moment of hunting his prey was the best part of taking the life of innocent blood.

* * * *

As Alydia and Simon were about to turn the corner, when suddenly Simon noticed a strange man following them. Curiously, Simon looked behind him in the crowd of the lingering townspeople and noticed that the man was gone. *What was that?* He thought to himself. Thinking that he was just being suspicious, he continued walking alongside Alydia.

Knowing the journey for them would be long, Simon looked at Alydia and asked her to get a loaf of bread for the journey from Marie's Boulangerie.

"And where will you be going?" Alydia asked.

"I know few folks that could give us directions, many things have changed since we were back home."

* * * *

Leonardo knew that this was his chance to reach out to Lexa. He soundlessly followed her footsteps into the bakery. Stepping into the quaint bakery of the town, the aroma filled his mind. It wasn't the aroma of the freshly baked dough but of the girl. Her human odor filled the store and triggered his thirst, yet something about her scent was familiar to him.

"Bonjour monsieur, how can I serve you? the baker asked, distracting his thoughts. "I am fine, thank you. I have everything I need," Leonardo replied, barely acknowledging the baker.

Alydia roamed through the bakery shop, comforted by the aromas and the beautiful displayed pastries. It reminded her about the pastries that her mother used to bake every morning. The smell of fresh dough brought warmth to her heart, that made her eager to taste some. In the midst of her eagerness, she was distracted by a presence staring at her. Taken by surprise at his appearance, Alydia turned to acknowledge Leonardo, when she suddenly felt a familiar ambiance about him.

"Hello," Leonardo finally said as he looked into her beautiful blue eyes.

"Have we met before?" she asked.

A gradual smile formed across Leonardo's lips, and he gave her a moment to think about where she might have seen him.

"I met you at Le Paradis de L'enfer a year ago, didn't I?"

"Yes."

"How did you find me here?"

"Your friend Sheryl mentioned that you were heading back to Pittsburgh, and now it seems that our paths happened to cross," Leonardo explained.

"Who are you?" she finally asked.

"Do you truly want to know who I am?" Leonardo said, taking one step closer to her.

"Yes ... I do," she said as she stood inches away from him, not afraid of how close he was getting.

"I am just a man who has fashioned an interest since the day I caught a glimpse of you working in the tavern. My dear, you seem so different and alluring," Leonardo explained, witnessing her cheeks turn a shade of rose.

As she was giving into his seductive charms, Leonardo gently reached his hand out toward her warm, delicate hand. She felt his cold hand against her skin and sensed a familiar yet distant connection with him. Nevertheless, she didn't have a clue about who he really was and where he came from, but deep within, it felt as if she had known him in another life. Diverting her thoughts, the baker came from the back with a fresh loaf of bread and interrupted their conversation. Leonardo quickly pulled away from her and took care of the payment.

"My treat."

"No thank you, there is no need."

"I insist."

Staring down at Leonardo, the baker took his money, knowing that he didn't care where the money came from, just as long he got his money in the end.

Leonardo and Alydia walked out of the bakery and stood before each other along the dimly lit street.

"Thank you, for the kind gesture. It was very nice of you," She said.

"It was my pleasure," Leonardo replied.

Looking past his pale demeanor and into his dark emerald eyes, she was reminded of her lost brother who had similar eyes of sadness. "Please, sir, tell me who you are," Alydia said, puzzled at why he paid for her purchase and why he had an interest in her.

As the night breeze blew between them, her fragrance boiled the quenched thirst that burned inside of his cold, dead body. He did not want to reveal his name just yet, but his attraction to her overpowered his wishes.

"My name is Leonardo—"

"Are you ready to go?" Simon said, interrupting Leonardo as he walked down the street toward them.

With her creased brow and stunned expression upon her face, Alydia turned around to see Simon coming her way. As she turned back to ask Leonardo more questions about who he was and where he came from, he was gone.

"You okay? You look a little pale," Simon said, troubled about what he had just walked into.

"Yes … I was just speaking to … I mean, he was standing right here. This man came into the bakery to find out more about me. He even paid for the bread," Alydia said, stumbling on her words and trying to grasp what had just happened.

"And, he just vanished?"

"Well … yes … I guess so," she replied, coming to terms with reality.

"I see. Well, we can't wait around for this mysterious man to show up again. We have quite a journey ahead of us."

Alydia and Simon gathered their things and continued on their way.

XIII

Leonardo knew better than to get another person involved in his hunt to kill, especially with a prey as intriguing as Lexa. He decided to hide from her friend by going into the back alley of the bakery. He wanted her all to himself, but at the opportune moment when there would be nowhere or no one to hide from. Besides, Leonardo knew that this wouldn't be the last time he would see her, for his emotionless stone heart yearned for her scent and her innocent blood. Her voice consumed his thoughts, and her beautiful mortal face was the only image that came to mind. With his taken mind, Leonardo knew what he had to do.

*　　*　　*　　*

Along the road, Alydia and Simon traveled in silence. Simon was focused on where they needed to go and what lay ahead once they reached their destination. Alydia was still thinking about the man she had encountered at the bakery.

He said his name was Leonardo, Alydia thought. She was confused yet intrigued.

Simon turned to Alydia and was concerned with what was going on in her mind. He was hesitant to ask but knew something or someone was troubling her thoughts.

"Alydia, what's wrong? Why do you look so troubled?"

"Did you ever know the truth behind my brother?" Alydia asked as she finally looked up at Simon.

"You mean Leonardo?"

"Yes. Did you know that my mother found him when he was just a baby? He was abandoned along the river by our house, and my mother said that one day she heard his cries and knew from her motherly intuition that he had been left to live on his own in this big world. She took him in and decided to raise him as her own child. She taught him everything—how to walk, talk, and be the man he could've been today."

"Oh, I didn't know that about Leonardo. However, I do remember how much Joyce loved him, just like my mother loved David and me. May they rest in peace."

"However, the fact of the matter is that my father never loved Leonardo; he never gave him the attention or love that he deserved. Knowing that my brother was not of my own blood and no matter where he came from, I loved him. My brother taught me to be strong, and I came to learn about having a big heart," Alydia continued to say.

They both stood there, processing what was being said. Simon took Alydia's hands to comfort her and to show that he was there for her.

Alydia looked up and searched Simon's eyes for an answer about how she was going to bring herself to say the next words.

"Simon … I think the man I just met was my brother. It was Leonardo," Alydia said, without any regret in what she was saying.

"Do you have any idea what you are saying, Alydia? That would be impossible."

"No, it's not. Something about his presence was familiar. I could feel it."

"If that was Leonardo, then why now? Where has he been all this time? How did he manage to survive?" Simon persistently asked.

"I don't know, Simon, but that was him!" Alydia yelled, but it seemed that the more she tried to explain herself, the less Simon believed her.

Taking a deep breath to give himself patience, Simon said, "The man you saw today was not your brother."

"He is, Simon!"

"No, Alydia! Leonardo is dead!" Simon finally yelled back.

All was silent again except the chirping of crickets and winds that traveled. Alydia didn't know what else to say to convince Simon, so she decided to keep her thoughts to herself.

Moments later, Simon again felt that someone was following them. To try to get rid of whoever was following them, he took Alydia's arm and immediately pulled her into the nearby woods. Moving further and further into the wilderness, Alydia tried to stop him, trying to pull herself away and asking why they were heading into the woods.

"I believe we are being followed," Simon said.

"But why can't we just find a shelter in town? Do you think it's safe in the woods?" Alydia asked frightened.

"I honestly trust the woods more than being in town at the moment."

"Are you sure, Simon?"

"Just trust me," Simon replied as they continued through the woods.

Simon knew the way around the woods better than anyone else, but he was determined to figure out what this man wanted from them, so he decided to keep moving on instead of stopping to rest.

"We will continue on till morning. That way we can make it home by dawn," Simon stated.

"But we need to rest, Simon. Besides, it is too dark to see in the woods," Alydia replied. "It will be hard for me to keep up with you."

Realizing that Alydia was right, Simon let out a sigh of frustration. He looked around to find a big enough tree to rest for the night.

"Okay, we shall rest here, next to this redwood tree, but I'll keep my ears open for anything suspicious or anything that may be lurking within the shadows," Simon said. Alydia nodded in confirmation. They settled in against the tree until dawn, where they would then continue on with their journey.

*   *   *   *

Leonardo was keeping his distance behind them when he heard crackling of leaves and voices miles away, west of the forest. The sudden scent of new blood awakened his senses and made him thirst for it. He knew that Lexa and her companion would be resting for the night, so Leonardo made his way to the drunken strangers that had stumbled their way into the forest. Hunting for his prey among the darkness, he peered within the camouflaged leaves that hung from the trees. Leonardo saw two young women being pressured by their suitors to act upon their impure thoughts. Unfortunately, the young women were unaware of the predestined death that the men had planned for them. However, Leonardo knew about their intentions, as he had read their minds, but it didn't matter what their plans were because they were all destined to die tonight.

Aware that he needed his strength for the next night, Leonardo silently made his way to the crowd, as they had begun to fall into the sensual effects of lust and passion for one another. "Come here my darlings, we will show you what real men do," one of the men said, as one of the girls lustfully grabbed her own breasts. Just as the men were starting to unveil the nakedness of the innocent young women, it seemed that a strong gust of wind passed by them. Leonardo suddenly snapped one of the men's necks and bit the other man's neck, spilling blood vigorously over the grounds, and before the two young women could run away from fright, they were hypnotized by Leonardo's glare. *Don't run. Stand still and be silent,* he said to them subconsciously.

Leonardo could see that the women were trembling from the cold and from fright of seeing the blood being spilled onto the grounds of the forest. Yet he was pleased that they obeyed his command, as he could sense their confusion, since they were unable to understand why they couldn't break free from his spell. Leonardo stood before them, glaring at their innocent beauty, deciding what to do with them.

"Two beautiful ladies like you should not be fooling around in these parts of the woods," Leonardo said, with a cunning smile as he imagined the things he could do to them.

He could take their lives and be satisfied with the warmth of the blood flowing through his cold veins, he could make them kill each other until the light was gone from their eyes, or he could turn them into vampires, but he realized that he didn't have the strength or the knowledge to raise newborns.

"Should I let you run away to give you another chance to live? Or should I take your lives as punishment for you being so naïve?" Leonardo asked, playfully stroking the locks of their hair.

Dawn was approaching soon, and in a sudden blaze, Leonardo brought the young woman with raven hair up to her feet. Dazed by the veins appearing beneath her skin, he pulled her hair, making her head jerk back, and violently sunk his teeth into her neck. He drank her blood until her body went limp. Not quite satisfied for the night, he went for the wide-eyed, brown-haired woman that was trying to use all her strength to bring out a scream, but Leonardo's spell still overpowered her will. She too was dragged to her feet and drained of all her blood.

Now Leonardo was satisfied for the night. Wanting to give a cautionary warning to the townspeople for their lack of control and carelessness, he piled the bodies on top of each other near the outskirts of town. Once finished, Leonardo went back to where Lexa and her friend were resting for the night.

He knew that he couldn't survive the daylight by hiding in the shadows that the trees were to form. Being in the town was certainly risky, especially since the authorities could still be searching for the murderer of the priest and Mr. Cooper. Not having any other alternatives and knowing that there was no cave or an abandoned place for him to sleep during the day, Leonardo decided to dig himself a six-foot grave to sleep in during the day, near where Simon and Lexa were sleeping. It became his priority that by nightfall he would find Lexa by the invigorating scent of her blood, continuing his desire to get what he wanted. Nothing would get in his way.

✻ ✻ ✻ ✻

Miles away, when the dark sky had just a few more hours before daylight overpowered the night, a mysterious fog began to form, layering the grounds. Near the outskirts of the bordering town stood the town's watchman. Henry Dean, a forty-seven-year-old man who had watched over the town for the past twenty years, was walking through the sleeping town of Pittsburgh, looking for any usual activity. Henry walked miles around town every night with his rifle and a cigar, on the lookout for any kind of creature that could be lurking in the woods, wanting to harm his people. The story behind Henry was that he was part of a secret organization called the Dark Knights of the Ancient Order, founded by the Vatican centuries ago to hunt mystical creatures such as witches, vampires, and others creatures believed to be a part of the devil's work against God's laws. Henry's main purpose, which was designated by these so-called hunters, was to guard and protect the land of Pittsburgh. Even though there hadn't been many supernatural occurrences during the past nine years, the town knew that any sign of witchcraft being performed or any immortal beings lingering around and performing evil deeds within the town would be hunted down and brought to justice, where they would instantly be found guilty and sentenced to death.

As he continued the way around town, he noticed something out of place just a few feet away. Coming closer, he saw a pile of dead bodies covered in their own blood. Keeping a calm manner, Henry saw that the two women and two men lying in front of him were recently murdered. To any other person, it would seem that they were attacked and killed by an animal from within the dark forest; however, as he examined the bodies, he knew very well that they were not attacked by an animal but by a dark creature. Henry could see that their necks were pierced with two punctures wounds, and that all their blood had been drained from their bodies. Their skin was ice cold. This was definitely no work of witchcraft, which meant that a darker and more dangerous creature threatened the land of Pittsburgh.

"It cannot be. It's not possible!" Henry exclaimed in confusion.

Trying to figure out what kind of creature could have done this, Henry looked up to examine the forest for anything strange. Suddenly a dark figure seemed to be approaching him from the distance. Startled at the fact that this could be the creature, Henry hastily took out his rifle and shot in the direction of the oncoming figure, hoping to kill or wound it. As the smoke of the rifle cleared, it seemed that the figure vanished. Henry thought he was being paranoid from the stories he had heard before of deadly and heartless creatures that left dead bodies in their wake. Nevertheless, Henry knew he had to go into town immediately. He went to wake the others to inform them of the bodies he had found. Unfortunately, he was stopped in his tracks by the impression of someone following him. He could feel that the dark figure was back. Henry quickly turned around to see a hooded figure standing only inches away from him. Stepping back with fright, Henry demanded that the figure reveal who he was.

Fear swept through Henry's body as he realized who it was. Many believed him to be a myth for many centuries, but he and the Dark Knights knew that he was one of the few immortals they feared the most. They knew of his countless murders and dark stories of how he slaughtered innocent women and children through the ages.

"It's you," Henry said in barely a whisper, his throat going dry. "What are you doing here, Boris?"

"Hello to you too, old friend," Boris said.

"You were told to never come back here," Henry stated as he began to slowly reach for his rifle.

"Old habits, I suppose. You remember that you and I have an old score to settle?" Boris replied as he walked around Henry, examining how much he had aged over the years.

Henry quickly grabbed his rifle, but before he could bring it up to pull the trigger, Boris wrapped his long fingers around his neck, bringing his feet off the ground and staring him down.

"Now, now, Henry. Why would you go and do a silly thing like that? We both know you are no longer that same hunter who faced me years ago. Pity. I rather enjoyed our game. I believe now it is time to settle this matter once and for all. Wouldn't you agree?"

"Boris, when I depart from this world and you are still living in the hell you call life, someone, sooner or later, will finish what I started. By the holy order of—"

Not letting Henry finish his sentence, Boris's fangs set into Henry's neck, sucking his blood until Henry's screams of agony and pain stopped. Unhooking his fangs from Henry's neck, as he was still somewhat conscious, Boris looked at Henry with blood dripping from his mouth and laughed with great pride, as the score had finally been settled. Boris ripped his head off, instantly killing Henry, blood spilling like a broken water fountain, and left his decapitated body with the other dead bodies lying within the woods.

"So long, Henry. For years, you claimed to be above my power, and now you lay on the ground beneath my feet like cattle, nothing more than rotten flesh from your own past. Farewell, Dark Knight."

Boris looked up into the night sky, cherishing the blood that still lingered between his lips. He then opened his arms widely toward the sky in proclamation of his triumph and pride.

XIV

The next morning, Alydia was having a terrible nightmare about her family being killed, and she could hear their screams of brutal agony. She dreamt of how her brother was alone in the world as an outcast and how she saw herself running toward Leonardo in the middle of the dirty roads in town as he was walking away. "Leonardo!" She yelled out. As she ran to him, the daylight became night in a matter of seconds, and a drastic storm began to fall on them, but as she was only a few steps away from Leonardo, he turned around to face her. She was startled at what she saw; Leonardo had blood trickling from his mouth, and his hands were covered in blood. In his left hand, extended straight in front of him, he held his own beating heart. Alydia was trembling in fear. Leonardo stared into her eyes with hunger, as his own eyes turned from human into the eyes of a monster.

"There you are, my sweet sister," he said with a cunning smile. This entity who appeared before Alydia was not Leonardo; it was another man whose eyes where filled with darkness and whose skin was as pale as the moonlight. Afraid of what she saw, Alydia ran in the other direction until another appeared before her. It was Boris.

"Remember me?" Boris asked, stopping Alydia in her tracks.

Waking up in a sweat from the heat of the sun and from the horrible nightmare that had just occurred, Alydia was then startled by the crackling noise coming from nearby. With her eyes barely opening from sleep and the momentary blurriness that covered them, Simon was nowhere to be found. Panicked and anxious, Alydia quickly got up and shuffled to find a sharp enough stick to protect her. The crackling and rustling noise seemed to quicken and come nearer. Her heart began to quicken as the unknown creature hastened in speed. Suddenly, a rabbit leapt out of the woods but then suddenly dropped in midair, as it was shot from within the distance. Alydia gave out a shout from the abrupt thud of the rabbit, which now lay lifeless in front of her.

"There is no need to be frightened. I was just catching some breakfast for us," Simon said as he walked from the same direction that the rabbit was running from. "I am so sorry if I frightened you, Alydia. I meant to hunt yards away from here, and I didn't expect the rabbit to run toward you at full speed."

"You could have shot me, Simon."

"I'm sorry! I had to kill the rabbit before it got away. I—"

"Just forget it," Alydia said, looking away.

"Are you all right? You seem bothered by something else."

"I had a dream."

"Was it about your family again? Must've been a really bad dream for you to be frightened like this."

"I wasn't frightened . . . just startled from it, that's all."

"It was just a bad dream, Alydia, nothing to be worried about."

"I dreamt of my brother again, but it wasn't quite him. There was another man too, and he asked if I remembered him, but I didn't. Like you said, it was a dream after all." Alydia brought her knees up to her chest and hugged her arms close around her legs.

Simon began making their breakfast for the morning. Meanwhile, Alydia became thoughtful, playing back the moment of her encounter with the man at the bakery last night. She went and sat back down near the redwood tree, thinking of how that moment seemed to affect her past, present, and future. It was an odd feeling, but she now wondered what the future had in store for her as they moved closer to the one place she promised herself to never return to.

As Simon finished cleaning the rabbit and prepared to cook it, he asked why Alydia was so deep in thought. She shook her head, hiding her true feelings from Simon, because she knew he would continue to disagree with her about knowing that Leonardo was still alive.

Simon looked at her with pity and sorrow that she still held on to the thought of her lost brother. As he was forming a small fire from striking two rocks together, his thoughts continued, as he could not understand why she was putting herself through such agony for someone who no longer existed. Placing the dead rabbit over the fire, he contemplated about what they went through that night. He knew Leonardo was dead, because he was determined to believe that he could have never been able to survive what they went through that night long ago. Knowing that he was right, he looked over to Alydia, who was sitting and staring into the open woods. He realized that he had to protect her from whatever it was they were heading to.

Simon placed the cooked rabbit down upon some leaves to cool off and went over to Alydia to comfort her. "We will get through this together. Everything will be alright, I know it." He gently reached over and grabbed her hands, and as she turned and looked into his eyes, he could see in her eyes that there was no way to change her mind and that the only thing was for Alydia to see the truth for herself. Simon kindly got up and went to serve himself and Alydia rabbit for breakfast.

Eating in silence, they were both filled and content with the nourishment that the rabbit was able to give them.

"Alydia, what do you think you will find back home?"

"I don't know, Simon. Maybe I will be able to find hope."

Simon didn't know how to reply, but he felt that the hope she was seeking was long gone.

Having their fill, Alydia and Simon knew that it was time to continue on, so they began to clean up and gather the few things they had and start their journey into town.

Just as they had eaten in silence, they journeyed through the woods in silence, giving them much to think about. With miles behind them, a sudden noise emerged from ahead, and a flock of birds dispersed and flew over them above the trees. Alydia and Simon believed it to be nothing more than a sudden movement in the wind, but they were wrong. They both heard screams and loud ranting coming from townspeople up ahead. Turning and looking at each other to comprehend what they just heard, Alydia ran toward the townspeople, and before Simon could stop her from running into danger, he ran after her. "Alydia, wait!"

A huge crowd gathered around what seemed to be a pile of corpses. People were frightened, but most of all they all wanted justice for whoever did this unthinkable act, especially for Henry Dean, the man who had protected their land for years.

Once they reached the gathered crowd that stood on the border of Pittsburgh, Alydia quickly turned away, and bared her face into Simon's chest from fear at what she just witnessed. It was a horrifying sight, and even Simon couldn't believe this massacre that lay before them. "My goodness, who would do such a thing? This is appalling." He said in disbelief. It certainly brought them the unwanted memories of the death of their families. Whoever had done such abomination, they believed, was possessed with an evil entity.

As he was comforting her, a few people from the crowd noticed their appearance from the woods. "Excuse me, but what are you doing here, slave?" a man asked, holding his young daughter close to him.

"We come from the west to return to our hometown. My name is Simon, a lone slave from the Le' Muerte family, and this here is Alydia Le' Muerte, the last member of her family," Simon replied as Alydia looked up to give them a welcoming nod.

Whispers spread swiftly across the crowd, as if Simon had said something offensive.

From deep in the crowd, a middle-aged man came through to face them. He seemed to be a well-kept man, but what stood out was the limp he had in his left leg as he leaned against his cane.

"Did you say you were from the Le' Muerte family?" he asked in wonder.

Alydia looked at him with curious eyes and replied that she was the only daughter of Marco and Joyce Le' Muerte.

The man stood there as if seeing a ghost. "I knew your parents well, and the last time I saw you and your brother, Leonardo, you were just a child playing among the other children of your age. I am so sorry for the loss of your family, dear child."

Alydia didn't know what to say except thank you and to appreciate his well-mannered condolences. She didn't recognize the man but wondered how much he knew of her family and whether he knew if Leonardo was dead or alive.

Suddenly a little girl interrupted their conversation. "Did you come through the woods?" she asked, scared, pointing toward the woods.

"Yes, we did."

The people from the crowd looked surprised that two young individuals were able to manage the woods on their own.

"Well, I am afraid you have come at a bad time. There seems to be a killer on the loose, and it made its first attack last night," the father of the girl said.

"We are sorry for what's happening, and we know these are dark times, but we come to ask for shelter," Alydia said.

The people nodded with acknowledgment of their condolences.

"Is there a place that we can rest for the night?" asked Alydia in desperation.

An older woman, with her gray hair peeking out of her headscarf, turned to look at Alydia and Simon, and after a moment of contemplating, she said that she owned a small home with extra rooms a few blocks down from where they were, but she warned them that they could stay there only for the night.

They both nodded in thanks and gratitude and began their way as they followed the woman in silence. Entering into the town that they once called home, Alydia and Simon both could agree that the town had changed since they were last there as children. There were many more people from all over—blacksmiths, shoemakers, farmers, politicians, soldiers, all who had been coming from the far east colonies to help grow this promising land since its founding in 1758.

The Pittsburgh sign engraved in stone stood the same as always, as if it never aged or chipped away as years passed. The pine trees all grew the same way along the narrow path that formed the town, along with the tall mountains the protected the vast land. The houses were built side by side along the river bend that was filled with steamboats and fishermen. The biggest difference that Alydia and Simon could sense in the air was the smell of death and sadness from the war.

They were approaching a two-story redbrick house that stood in the middle of town. It was a house unlike any other along the street. Realizing that this was new to them, the old woman stopped them before entering through the front door and turned around to face them.

"Remember that you will be staying here for one night only."

"Yes, thank you. We will be out of your way by morning," Alydia replied.

Entering the strange house, Alydia and Simon could feel an unusual sense of secrecy but knew better than to ask questions of someone who was offering them a place to stay. The woman's house was simple, and nothing seemed out of the ordinary. The woman guided them to the second floor and presented their room at the end of the hall. She let them settle in while she headed back downstairs to make dinner for them.

Their room was small and quaint enough to satisfy their needs for the night.

"Finally, we can get a good night's rest," Simon stated.

"Yes, I hope so," Alydia said.

Confused by Alydia's reaction, Simon said, "I don't understand. What do you mean?"

Alydia shook her head, not knowing a way to explain how she felt about staying in the house. "I don't know, Simon."

"Either way, we will only be here for the night. Let us just be thankful that we have a place to stay," Simon said, feeling comfortable. "Besides, I'd rather be here tonight than out in the woods, especially after seeing those bloody corpses."

Alydia nodded in agreement, but deep down, she hoped that nothing would happen during their stay.

* * * *

Meanwhile, downstairs, the elderly woman began preparations to make dinner for her guests. Oddly enough, she realized that it was a coincidence that the last heir of the Le' Muerte still lived and was now staying in her house. For as long as she could remember, she wanted revenge on the Le' Muertes for what they did to her and her family. For years, she had never missed a night of thinking about what happened. When she heard of the death of the Le' Muerte family, she thought it was over. However, it was far from over, and she had plans for them both. What was most pleasing was that Alydia and Simon were unaware of what was to become of their lives, as they were both staying in the house of a dark witch.

* * * *

After washing up from their journey that they had endured, Alydia decided to rest her eyes before dinner was ready. Nightfall was approaching upon the land, yet the image of the man in her dreams was set in her mind and it didn't help that her thoughts were running wild. She was restless.

"What is wrong with me?" she asked, feeling worried.

"Nothing is wrong with you, Alydia," Simon said, sitting next to her and gently holding her hands and looking straight into her eyes.

Simon realized that she feared something great, for her skin went pale, and her body quivered from the thoughts stirring in her mind.

"You must stop worrying about all of this, Alydia. It is time to start thinking about your future."

"My future? What future do I have when my family's legacy has ended? This is why I keep holding on to the last shred of hope, believing that my brother may still be alive."

As she said this, Simon understood what she meant by holding something so dear to one's heart, no matter how far or near it might be. This was why he never left her side, even when she showed no kind of affection toward his feelings for her. Yet if she wanted a future, this was the opportunity for him to express his feelings, so that maybe with any hope, they would be able to move forward and start a future together.

With a long sigh, Simon brought his hand to her face to caress her soft skin.

"Alydia, if you want to move on and start your future, I can give that to you."

"What are you talking about, Simon?"

"Since we were children, my eyes and my heart have only wanted you. Don't you see, Alydia? I care for you so much that I would go to the ends of the world for you. My feelings, which have grown more over time, run deeper than any known love. I only wish that you could understand how much you mean to me. If only you knew how my heart skipped a beat every time you walk into a room. If only you knew the pain I go through when I see you like this. This is me giving you my heart, and I ask of nothing in return but your love. I may have nothing to give you, and I may come from a slave family, but I hope that my love and trust are enough to share a life with you. Alydia, this is my declaration of my love to you. I love you, and I will never stop loving you."

Alydia didn't know what to say. "Simon, your words were so kind, but I am—"

Before Alydia could explain to Simon that she didn't feel the same way toward him, the elderly woman came through the bedroom in a full rage after eavesdropping on their conversation.

"Don't tell me that you are in love with a Le' Muerte!" the woman cried out to Simon. "That family is cursed!"

Simon and Alydia stood up from the bed, startled by the woman's unwelcome outburst.

"You conniving little boy! How dare you love this girl who is from a family that took everything away from me."

Simon stepped in front of the woman to protect Alydia.

"The accusations that you are making, ma'am, are false. The Le' Muerte family are good people who have done no harm," Simon explained.

"No harm? Good people? Don't speak of things that you don't know of, boy!" The woman was in a fury. Before Simon could realize what was coming, her hand clawed across his face, causing his body to be thrown against the wall and slump down to the floor.

"Simon!" Alydia screamed, running to him to comfort him in his pain.

"He is a slave. He doesn't need your compassion, nor do either of you deserve it," the woman said in such a dark tone that Alydia could feel how wicked she was.

Suddenly, Alydia was gasping for air. With despair in her eyes, she turned toward the woman and was stunned that the woman was standing in the same place without a hand on her.

"How?" Alydia tried to say, in barely a whisper.

"You are asking the wrong question, my dear. You should be asking what you did."

To fulfill her sinister plan, Alydia needed to be kept alive. She released her from her grasp.

Every organ in her body appreciated every strain of air that was inhaled. Alydia felt as if she had finally reached the surface after suffocating within a deep, vast ocean.

"What do you want from me? I have done you no harm," Alydia said.

The woman didn't answer but simply, with an unknown force, brought Simon and Alydia up to their feet. Without understanding what was happening, they were being drawn by a power that forced them to follow the women down to the kitchen.

"You see, there is something you don't know about me, so you will sit down and listen." The woman made Alydia and Simon sit down against their will.

"When I was eight, my father and your father, Marco Le' Muerte, were close friends, almost like brothers. I was one of six siblings at the time, so I was able to sneak around and listen in on various conversations, with no one realizing that I was missing." As the woman was telling her story, she was mixing and throwing things into a brew that caused an unusual aroma to erupt. Without any attention toward the aroma clouding the house, the woman continued her story.

"Eventually, I became the keeper of secrets from all the whispers and rumors I overheard. One afternoon, I was helping Mama with the daily chores, and as I was sweeping the porch, a strange man was creeping around, seeming as if he didn't want to get caught, as he carried a small pounce and a familiar gun. The next day as I was playing in the fields, minding my own business, your father, Marco, came storming down to our house and started banging on the door."

Alydia and Marco jumped from the unexpected banging of the woman's fist against the countertop.

"Yes, just like that. It was a violent welcoming to our house. My father came out of the house, startled by Marco's outburst, wanting to know what all the commotion was about. 'You stole from me!' That is what he kept saying, over and over again. My innocent father stood there and explained with all his might that it wasn't him that he wouldn't steal from someone that he considered to be a brother. Marco wouldn't listen. He was a stubborn old man, and once he believed in something, he wouldn't let it go. I tried to explain to them about the wary man I saw, but of course, who would believe a child?"

The aroma in the house was getting stronger, which made Alydia and Simon delirious. "Can you feel your deepest, darkest fears flowing in your mind?" the woman asked.

"What are you?" Alydia asked, trying to avoid the power that was seeping through her. But it was too late; her vision was beginning to blur.

"Your curiosity will be answered soon enough," the woman said. "So, of course, no one believed what I had to say, and from that day on, our family name was tarnished. Marco had my father arrested, and after a few days, he died of a heart attack in prison. After that, we lost everything. Weeks later, mother was raped and murdered, and my siblings and I were forced to work and beg for money, until each of them passed away one by one, and now I am the only living member of my family."

The woman completed her brew and then walked over to Alydia to face her and reveal to her what and who she was.

"Since that day, I made an oath to take back the life that was stolen from my family. Now, as I have practiced dark magic over the years and evolved into a living witch, I can take the last living life of the Le' Muerte family."

The woman was inches away from Alydia's face, and she could tell that her magic was working by making her unwelcomed visitors feel a loss of control.

"Your seed shall no longer continue, and your family name will no longer exist!"

Without hesitation or fair warning, the woman forced her to look at Simon, as she was still inches away from Alydia's face. The woman raised her arm to her side and gradually turned her wrist sharply around. As she did this, Simon's torso simultaneously twisted around, breaking every bone and ending his life.

With the aroma of the brew still clouding her mind, Alydia was in shock at the horror she had just witnessed. Terror ran through her body, making her frozen and speechless in her place. She wanted to scream, but words were unable to form against her lips. The only awareness that came to mind was that she knew she had to escape.

The witch stood up and took a step back to examine the situation. Satisfied with her act of cruelty, she suddenly grabbed Alydia by the hair and began to pull her across the house. With tears of pain, Alydia struggled to become free of the witch's grasp. She tried to grab hold of anything within her path to prevent whatever plan the witch had in store for her.

"Come on, you silly girl! No one and nothing will be able to help you now."

"Please let me go!"

As she was being dragged across the floor, Alydia saw blood running down the walls and began to consume everything that she tried to grasp onto. The witch took her outside to the open grave that awaited her. Alydia struggled to free herself from her grasp, but the unnatural strength of the witch was too strong for her. As she was being dragged by her hair and being push and pulled like a ragdoll, Alydia began to hear disembodied voices lingering in the air. It was as if these poor souls were being mutilated and tortured.

"What you see is the blood of all my victims, everyone that I killed in order to get to you, including your dear Simon, the slave who loved you oh so dearly. This is all the blood that you shed!" the woman said, feeling gratified that her plan was coming into place as she had dreamt for many nights.

Alydia couldn't form any words to describe what she saw, nor could she comprehend the number of victims that had been killed in her name.

On the verge of giving up all hope, Alydia was finally dragged into the woods. The woman finally released Alydia's hair and left her lying next to the grave she was going to be buried alive in, as she had placed a brutalizing curse upon the grave. The woman turned away for a second, and Alydia knew that this was her chance. She gathered all the strength she had and grabbed a fistful of dirt. As soon as the woman turned around, Alydia threw the dirt in her face.

The woman cried out in distress. "You stupid girl!"

This was it. Alydia brought herself to her feet and with the only thing she had to live for, she began to run as far away as she could.

XV

As darkness finally fell upon the town, it was time for Leonardo to continue his journey. He broke out from the ground, awakened from his slumber, knowing exactly what he had to do. As if his body and clothes were immune to dirt, he stood up without a speck of filth on him. Breathing in the fresh air, he realized that something was missing. The scent of Lexa was close to gone. With great speed, Leonardo headed in her direction, as he was able to pick up her succulent scent. He inhaled her scent, making him grow more eager to see her. *It's our time now,* he thought to himself. However, as he got closer, he could feel that something was wrong. He could smell fear and an unknown entity that did not belong.

Approaching the town of Pittsburgh, Leonardo noticed a young child sleeping beneath a lone tree. Leonardo looked down upon the girl, casting a dark shadow over her, and curiously wondered how the girl got to this place in her life. At the same time, he smiled upon her, knowing that there was nothing better than to start the night with fresh blood after sleeping all through the day. He kneeled down next to the girl and simply stared at her gentle, breathing body. The young girl woke up being confused and afraid, of her vision coming into focus from the late night. The girl with ripped clothes and a starved body began to cry to Leonardo as if he could save her from her miserable life. She cried for safety, but Leonardo knew that there was no point in her cries, no matter what caused her to be sleeping under the tree.

"Please, sir! Save me! Help me to have what you have. Please, sir, I beg of you!" the young girl cried out, trying to grab onto Leonardo.

Leonardo backed away from her, feeling disgusted. Leonardo saw himself in her as a worthless, filthy peasant. She moved further toward Leonardo and dropped down to her feet in the dirt, doing what she could to reach hold of Leonardo's cape with her dirty hands.

"Please, sir, help me! I know that I am worthless and useless to everyone, but please save me!"

Leonardo bent over toward the girl, and instead of sinking his fangs into her neck, he grabbed her face, making her look into his vampire eyes.

"Leave now and do not return. Stop with your cries, and if I find you here again, you will have no one to save you." Leonardo left the young girl alone and frightened.

Walking away from her made him feel anger. Why did he not feed on her? Leonardo knew that he wasn't the same man he was a year ago. Turning around he spotted the frightened girl running away further into the woods. He smiled with pride. Memories began to flare in his mind of when he was just a newborn vampire walking into the castle of the elders. He knew that if they saw him today, all their gossiping and doubts would be in vain, and they would owe him an apology. The vampires and Romulus would soon bow down to him.

Heading deeper into the town, Leonardo could hear a heart beating rapidly in fear in the distance, and he could feel the dark entity again, but this time it was stronger.

He sped toward the heartbeat when suddenly he stopped in his tracks, realizing it was Lexa running away from something within the woods.

Not looking where she was running, Alydia ran into Leonardo just standing there in the middle of the road.

Frightened, she looked up, and to her surprise, she was relieved that it was the mysterious man once again.

"My dear, why so frightened?" Leonardo asked, pleased to have her in his grasp.

She didn't know what to tell him. Would he believe her? So much happened in such little time.

"There you are, you little bitch!" the woman exclaimed as she came stammering from the woods. "How dare—" She stopped herself when she saw Leonardo.

A low growl blossomed from deep within Leonardo's throat. He pushed Lexa behind him to protect her. Leonardo's eyes turned into those of a vicious animal, with his fangs gleaming underneath his stare.

"A Vampire?" The witch said.

His growl began to come through his lips, and the witch knew that she had no choice but to run. "I suggest you run," he said in a menacing tone. She knew that she had no chance against a vampire.

"I will get my revenge on you soon and end your bloodline, if you're not already dead by then!" the witch said as she turned her back toward them and disappeared along with her house, as if she had never existed in the town.

Confused as to why a witch was after Lexa, Leonardo couldn't quite figure out what was going on, for he didn't possess enough power yet to fully understand this change in the winds.

"Come now. You are safe with me," Leonardo said to Alydia, bringing her around from behind him.

Not knowing how to feel, Alydia came around and stared out into the void where the witch's house once was.

"Where is your slave? Or companion?"

"Dead," was all Alydia could say from shock at the events that had just occurred.

The streets where empty, as no townsperson was awake at this time of night, and if they had heard any sound of distress, they knew to mind their own business.

Leonardo watched as Alydia walked over to the vacant space, and he could feel her pain for her companion. Reading her thoughts, he saw how the witch killed Simon.

Alydia felt that she had to do something in Simon's name, but there was no body for her to bury; it was gone along with the witch.

She suddenly turned toward Leonardo, realizing who came to her safety once again.

"It's you, Leonardo," she said in a whisper, walking up to him.

She knew it was her lost brother, but he looked so different. He looked dead.

"Are you alive?" Alydia asked.

"Yes, I am very much alive. Just as alive as you are right now," Leonardo replied.

"You don't remember me, do you?"

"Of course, I do. Your name is Lexa. We met at the old tavern where you were working."

Alydia's hope vanished, and her face fell in disappointment. He had no idea who she was, nor who he was. She knew that she had to do something to make him remember his life again. Something wasn't right about this man who stood in front of her. Leonardo acted so cold, and his stare was not that of the charismatic and loving young boy she once knew. His gestures where not his own, and his soul was not of a human. Alydia knew that Leonardo had been raised as a farm boy and not as a wealthy child, so how did it seem as if he was a man of high class, so well mannered? It was clear to her that the Leonardo she knew and the man who stood in front of her were different people yet one and the same.

"What are you?" Alydia asked, slightly frightened of the answer.

"If you knew what I am, not only would you not understand it, but you would run from it." Without hesitation, and knowing well enough that it was against all the Vampyr laws, a power took over, and he said, "Fallen from grace, rejected by the heavens, feared and wanted by all ..."

Leonardo looked down toward the stone that made the road and then looked at her with a silent stare. "I am a vampire."

She didn't know what to say. However, she knew that anything was possible, since her close encounter with death and the witch.

"Are you going to kill me?" Alydia asked, even though she felt in her heart that he wasn't going to hurt her.

Alydia made up her mind. The only place where she would ever have a chance of bringing Leonardo back was the one place they used to live together so many years ago.

"I must go now," Leonardo said, realizing that he had just put her in horrible danger. Without hesitation, he disappeared in the night, whispering in the wind that he would see her very soon, before the night ended.

For a brief moment, Alydia shed tears for him, realizing that her sense of resolve had become stronger, and knowing that when she and Leonardo reunited once again, the truth would be revealed. Nothing was going to stand in her way.

XVI

It was the last thing he wanted to do. He never wanted to put Lexa's life in harm's way, especially from the Dominus covenant. Breaking the Vampyr laws in such a way became an unbearable awareness he couldn't fully comprehend. Leonardo had vanished into one of the town's brothels. He felt that he needed to release his inner emotions and get wasted with fresh blood of the wicked. It was late at night, but the ladies always seemed to be working. Immediately, with his seductiveness, he was given the best woman on the job, who was soon going to satisfy his thirst.

Like any brothel, the room was filled with exotic colors and fabrics to hypnotize the men and women who entertained their imaginations. Entering the room, Leonardo turned toward the raven-haired woman and told her to wait for him at the bed, and so she went.

Pouring wine into a glass for the woman's nerves, he quickly turned around as he felt an unwelcomed visitor enter into the room.

"You! What are you doing here?" Leonardo asked, his voice full of hatred.

It was Boris, the vampire he least expected to see.

"Of all the people, Leonardo, you are upset with me? After all, you are the one who broke the most precious law of the Vampyr."

"You know, I was quite enjoying my life without you interfering all the time. Yet here we are once again."

Boris walked up to Leonardo and grabbed the glass of wine from his hand. "I completely forgot how sweet wine tastes like. I have never had the chance to drink anything else, except for what really satisfies and brings peace to my vampire tastes."

Boris gave the wine to the woman, who now believed she would be making love to two men. This excited her, and she drank the wine in one swift gulp and put the glass on the bedside table. She walked past Leonardo and made her way to Boris, where she gradually began to untie and unbutton his clothes.

He grabbed her wrist to make her stop. She was frightened, but she knew she had to please him. Boris began to kiss her palm and went toward her wrist, where he held her tight to puncture her skin. He grabbed the now empty glass and filled it with her blood. She wanted to scream at the sight of her own blood being drawn out, but Boris used his powers to keep her quiet.

"Where is she?" Boris asked, enjoying the thirst of warm blood.

Leonardo would do anything to protect Lexa, and he knew that Boris had yet to challenge him with his newfound strength. With grace and patience, Leonardo walked toward the whore who was now sitting upright on the bed, trying to stay strong from the blood she was losing. He grabbed her lifeless arm, bringing her up to her feet. With all his might, he thrusted his hand into her chest and took out her now lifeless heart.

"You see, Boris, since we last spoke, things have changed," Leonardo stated, squeezing the heart of every ounce of blood into the glass that Boris held.

No vampire had ever had such will within his hands, unless he was a vampire of many years. Leonardo's power was stronger than an ordinary newborn.

"How selfish and ignorant of you to do that, Leonardo. We could have shared her. I could still easily kill you without a care in the world for being such a worthless and insignificant newborn. No, tonight is not your night, my dear friend. Tonight, is her night. Death will be at her door once again."

"She belongs to me!"

Leonardo quickly charged at Boris, grabbing his neck and pushing him against the wall across the room. Boris was quite surprised to feel the hold of Leonardo, and realizing his new strength, Boris was at the moment of decapitation.

"That's enough, Leonardo. Don't forget you will be sentenced to immediate death if the elders find out you killed me." With hesitation, Leonardo let go.

"This isn't over. Until next time." Boris disappeared from the room.

Leonardo knew that he had to get to Lexa before Boris or any other vampire could. He too vanished from the brothel and went on his way as he heard cries of fear and death filling the air in the distance.

* * * *

Meanwhile, Alydia made her way to the end of the town, to the abandoned house that stood for many years, unoccupied. It was the house she grew up in and the house that changed everything. "I made it." Alydia said to herself. She stood in front of her home that once was surrounded by various flowers that she and her mother gardened together. Sadness filled her heart, for it reminded her of the love and memories that were once shared within the walls of their house. Now, no one dared to stay in a place that was covered in years of blood and had a bad omen. With all her strength, she stepped inside, hoping that her mother was in the walkway waiting to embrace her in her arms. Just like every night when she thought of her family, she realized it was only a dream. Alydia gently paced through, hoping that Leonardo would come to her once again. Maybe this was the place that would bring back the memories of who he was.

Going from room to room, Alydia remembered how she used to play and watch her mother cook and keep up with the house chores. Gliding her fingers against the chairs in the living area that were now covered in cobwebs and dust, it reminded her of when she and Leonardo were once held by their mother's arms to comfort them when they were sad, or when she would tell them funny stories to cheer them up. She then visited the room that was once the heart of the house, where her mother would make fresh bread in the morning with warm milk. Where her father would bring home deer and rabbit for dinner, he mother would put together a delicious feast every evening for the family. Alydia missed her father very much as well. She remembered how her father would carry her in his strong arms every time she fell asleep, and how her mother would sew clothes for them by the chimney every night before bedtime. "Mama, papa, I miss you so much," she said in sorrow. Now in place of the chimney sat the nest for a family of rats, huddled together from the cold.

Taking one step at a time, Alydia walked up the stairs, stained by the blood of her dead family. The scent of gore and death filled her nostrils, and she used all her might to hold back overwhelming tears. When she reached outside of her parents' bedroom, she saw the image of them on the floor, covered in their own blood. Alydia could even remember how her father struggled and fought with a mysterious man covered in black after killing her mother. She could still feel the anger and retaliation that the man had toward her father when her father held up a wooden stake toward the man. During that time, she could hear their servant Chloe screaming for her children's safety.

Why would someone attack our family? What have we done to deserve such crimes? Alydia still could not understand why this had to happen. Did the past of her father or mother come back to haunt them?

After turning away from her parents' bedroom, she went toward the bedroom she once shared with Leonardo. Lying on the floor next to her bed was her favorite childhood doll. She picked up the doll that was cloaked with dust, as it was now part of the history of the house; she remembered that she was so attached to her doll that she would never let it out of her sight. Alydia realized that she had grown up so much since then.

Making her way back downstairs with her old doll in her hand, she sat in the chair that her mother once sat in and waited for her brother to come back to her. "Leonardo, come back to me," she said.

✻ ✻ ✻ ✻

Concerned for Lexa's safety from Boris, Leonardo swiftly made his way to the abandoned house at the end of the town, where he could sense her scent. As he got closer to her, Leonardo could feel her pain, fear, and sadness.

It was known that when a mortal being went through turmoil of emotions, any vampire was able to find their prey. At this moment, Leonardo's full attraction to her was so strong that he could feel her clearly in his mind, a feeling he had never felt before during all his time as a newborn. He knew he had to get to her now—and quickly—before anything could happen to her.

As he was speeding to her, he looked up toward the sky with fortitude and purpose and felt a flow of passion rush through his body. He spread out his arms, as if asking for the night sky to take him away into the darkness. Leonardo closed his eyes, feeling the overwhelming change welcoming him. As if his body knew what to do naturally, his feet began to lift off from the ground, and his body began to soar. His speed heightened, and he knew what had just occurred. An incredible gift and power that was only obtained through time and patience was now within Leonardo's abilities. He was now in flight among the many ghosts that roamed against the night stars.

The night was quiet tonight, unusually so. Leonardo could sense in the winds that he was not going be alone tonight. He could smell blood and death following him as he flew toward the abandoned house. The closer he got to the house, the consciousness of death amplified. He realized that his past was trying to emerge through his thoughts and break his strength. Memories of bloodshed and screams surrounded him. Leonardo fought his way through with anger and blood thirst as his feet finally touched the ground and gracefully landed in front of the house. His eyes were now set for his one and only precious jewel.

☆ ☆ ☆ ☆

Peacefully, Alydia continued to wait for the return of her brother. Doubts began to cloud her feelings. Was Leonardo the man she once called brother? Was her mind playing tricks on her once again, or was it her nightmares finally haunting her reality? The only movement that arose within the room was the dust that floated inside the rays of the moonlight that peaked through the windows. As if the house was coming to life, the voice of a young boy crept through the walls and began to whisper to her.

Come back. Why did you leave me here to die?

Alydia was stricken with shock. She immediately stood up with a chill running down her spine as her childhood doll fell from her lap.

"Leonardo?"

Help me please, dear sister.

Was he truly alive? The voice came so clearly to her, and she followed the cries that led her outside to the front of the house.

She stood frozen right beneath the entryway of the terrace and to her disbelief saw Leonardo standing only a few feet away, a menacing look in his eyes.

She felt happy to see him again so soon but also feared him, for she did not understand what he truly was. Nevertheless, she couldn't comprehend why she felt that this was the moment she had been waiting for all her life.

"It is not safe for you to be out this late and so far from home, Lexa. You never know who may find you in the dark."

"Leonardo?" Alydia asked.

"Yes, it is I," Leonardo replied.

"I have been waiting for you all this time."

"Oh, my sweet child, I know you have. I have been waiting for you too, but now I am here."

135

Alydia gradually began to approach Leonardo. He felt so gratified that she was safe and that now he finally had her all to herself. He grabbed her warm hands and caressed them against his cold face.

"I have been waiting for this moment ever since I saw you."

Tears began to form in Alydia's eyes as she looked down in embarrassment.

"What's the matter?" Leonardo asked, gently pushing away the tears that fell down her cheek.

"Ever since I lost you years ago, Leonardo, I knew deep in my heart that you were alive. I never gave up on you."

Leonardo stared at her beautiful, opaque eyes. He noticed that her lips were constricted to hold back all her tears and overflowing emotions. Leonardo didn't understand what she was talking about. Confused, his eyes followed her hands that now moved to grab his hands.

"Tell me, why are you so cold and pale? Why do you look at me so?"

Trying to make her understand, Leonardo explained, "My dear Lexa. I am no ordinary man. I am the nightmare of all creatures but fiercer and stronger than any ordinary man. I do not fear death any longer, yet in turn, daylight will never appear on my flesh again. I am a monster that belongs to the darkness of the wicked and damned for eternity."

"I don't understand. You say you are a vampire. You say that you are a monster. But it doesn't have to be that way! All my life, I have sacrificed and suffered, searching for you. You are not the things you say you are! You are Leonardo Le' Muerte. You are my brother, and I am your sister, Alydia Le' Muerte!"

Baffled, Leonardo didn't know if this young woman was crazy or delirious. For a brief moment, he searched her face, for he knew that there was no one that really knew his full name, a name he had long forgotten since he had chosen his new life.

"I hid from the world as Lexa to protect our bloodline, but then you came and protected me from the witch. Don't you see, Leonardo? It was fate that brought us back together as family."

Without warning, Alydia put her arms around him, hugging him tightly to make sure that she wouldn't lose him again.

"You are my brother, the only family that I have left. I love you!" Tears were now pouring down Alydia's face, as she felt that she finally had made him realize the truth of his past.

Leonardo finally felt every inch of her warm body touching his cold body. With as much tenderness as he could bear, he put his hands around her and simply laid his head upon hers. Leonardo knew that this was how he was going to gain her trust and her affection to make her his. He had craved all of her since her sweet scent tore at his thirst for blood. He gently pushed her hair away to reveal her bare neck, waiting for the opportune moment to finally push his fangs into her. It was time to continue on with his plan. Leonardo firmly grabbed her by the shoulders and pushed her away from him. He kept her at arm's length for a moment to stare at the beauty of her eyes and rose-colored cheeks. Her blood ran through, which made Leonardo more enchanted with her scent. His eyes turned vampiric, and his gaze turned from seduction to that of a hunter, as it did with all his victims before.

In an instant, everything abruptly changed. Leonardo sensed a presence coming forth, a presence that he hoped wouldn't return. Alydia could see in Leonardo's face that something was wrong.

"What's wrong?" she asked.

Leonardo did not respond but instead immediately turned around to shield Alydia from what was coming.

"It's you again, Boris."

"Nice to have found you once more, and with her no less," Boris said, coming out of the shadows and into the moonlight for them to see.

Boris made his way toward Leonardo, pleased to see that his once newborn had made it this far on his own.

"Boris, how did you find me?" Leonardo asked.

"I will always know where you are and what you will be doing next, Leonardo. You should never forget that I am the one who made you."

"All this time and not a word from you. Tell me, Boris, how is your beloved Tabitha?"

"No need to change the subject. She is not of your concern."

"How can she not be? You left me for her, as I recall it. Though, I do thank you because I am now doing well for myself, compared to being your pawn."

"I knew when I turned you, Leonardo, that you were something special. Look at you. Your strength has grown exponentially, that the other vampires would envy you," Boris replied proudly.

Consumed by his hatred for Boris, for a brief moment Leonardo forgot that Alydia was with them.

"What is this, Leonardo? What is going on?" Alydia cautiously asked.

Leonardo turned around to face her and to read the thoughts of confusion and curiosity floating through her mind.

"Everything will be all right. Do not be afraid. You are safe with me."

With hatred turning into anger, Leonardo turned back toward Boris again and knew that he had to face his master once and for all.

"Ah ... she smells so sensual. I know now why you had trouble killing before; you were looking for her. Unless, of course, my dear friend is willing to share."

Boris made his way from Leonardo to Alydia. He could feel his body longing for her blood, as much as Leonardo could. As a lion protecting its cubs, Leonardo came between Boris and Alydia, making Boris understand that he was not willing to share his prey. Boris dismissed Leonardo's actions and instead grabbed Leonardo and pushed him to the side so that he could grab hold of Alydia. Leonardo was thrown with a force that caused him to knock down a tree that stood for many years.

Alydia now understood the magnitude of strength that Leonardo and Boris held. She ran back inside the house, frightened at what could happen. Yet, as she rushed back to safety, Boris laughed, for he thought she was foolish to think that running inside the house was going to save her. "There is no place to hide, my dear!" He said in a ominous laughter.

Leonardo charged toward Boris, slamming him into the ground, making a deep crater in the earth.

With amusement, Boris picked himself up. "You think you can kill me! It is time to finally learn your lesson!"

They both stood in a standstill, ready to strike at any given moment. Boris looked deep within Leonardo's thoughts and could feel his strength growing as the anger brewed inside.

Leonardo didn't hold back this time. He knew Alydia was back in the house, so it was time to take his full revenge on Boris. A great thunder filled the skies, making all the birds and creatures run away. Leonardo and Boris were entangled in a fight of speed and strength. More craters were formed in the ground. Strong trees began to fall like dying animals, but the most horrific sounds of this epic battle were the crackles and snarls of Leonardo and Boris. Both fought with anger from deep within, of pain from their past, and with one thought in mind—to kill or be killed. In a brief moment, Boris grabbed a nearby huge tree, picked it up and attacked Leonardo with great force. Leonardo stood his ground firmly, using his arms to defend himself from the tree, and like a twig, the tree splintered in half.

"You can do better than that, Boris!" He said.

Boris was amused and impressed by his prodigy's strength. "That was just a little taste of what I have to offer Leonardo. The worst has yet to come."

Leonardo and Boris knew that they weren't going to give up their lives or the life of precious Alydia; they were going to fight till the end, even if it was against the laws of the Vampyr.

Leonardo heaved Boris through the woods, and he landed at the steps of the house. He caught a long, thoughtful glimpse of Alydia as he got up once again to continue the battle.

"Interesting," Boris said.

Alydia was standing behind the door, not knowing whether to run as far away as she possibly could or wait for Leonardo to protect her from the monster that now stood in front of her. She knew what she needed to do. Instantaneously, as she turned to leave through the back of the house, Boris stood in front of her, blocking her path.

"I remember you. It was years ago, but now I know who you are," Boris said.

"You must be mistaken, sir. I have never—" Alydia's body was in shock. Everything froze in place, yet it moved a thousand miles a minute.

"Yes. How could I forget such radiant, warm skin and captivating eyes? We were once here together so many years ago. You were so innocent then," Boris said, reaching out to caress her.

"You were the one. You monster!"

"Quiet now, my child. There is no need to reminisce in the past. What's done is done."

Alydia began to feel a wave of emotions, in a state of astonishment that she didn't realize this sooner. Through her vulnerability, Boris was now able to hypnotize her under his powers. He touched her angelic face and moved his thumb gently across her quivering lips. A wave of faintness and nausea went through Alydia, but Boris only cared about taking her life in revenge of Leonardo. Under his spell, she could not move, nor could she speak to call out for help. She closed her eyes, as she was finally giving up on her own life.

Boris accepted her will. He was now inches from her face, mesmerized by her beauty. He placed his lips onto hers and gave her a passionate kiss that she had yet to experience in her life. Feeling such pleasure throughout their bodies, she let go and freed herself to Boris's seduction. His kisses moved away from her lips and gradually fell downward upon her flawless neck. Before Leonardo knew it was too late, Boris sank his fangs into her and made her blood innocent no more. Boris finally felt that Alydia was his, as her warm blood went through his veins and satisfied his body like human blood had never done before.

Alydia at first seemed to feel great pleasure from Boris, but as he held onto her more, the pain of loss began to emerge. Memories rushed over her of the horrible night that she had endured. As more of her blood was being drawn, flashbacks came of Boris drinking her mother's blood and the struggle her father went through to try and stay alive to protect his family. Boris was there that night when everything changed. Boris was the one who killed her family and left her to live her life alone, and now he had taken Leonardo, her only living family, away from her. It was too late though; her blood was now upon Boris's lips, and her body was now lifeless.

For a passing moment, Boris gently pulled away from her neck and looked into her dying eyes one last time.

"This is our true nature, and it will never change so as long as our species continues to exist."

Suddenly, Alydia could feel the release of Boris's grip, as she now was lying on the floor in the living room of the house. Leonardo hastily came to her to save the remaining life she had left within her. Boris was pushed away furiously against the wall, on the verge of breaking it down.

"You take her life, and I shall take your life in return!" Leonardo protested.

'You don't get it do you, Leonardo? You are still so ignorant! You will never learn that this is who we are!"

Boris grabbed Leonardo, and before he could attack, Leonardo quickly threw his fist into his chest and sent him roaring through the house and into the small cabin that stood behind the house. The smell of gas immediately erupted, as Leonardo did not realize that he had thrown Boris into barrels of thick liquid.

"Is this what you want for me to be? Drenched in product waste?" Boris asked. "For centuries, I have never had another vampire defy me, and just when

I created a newborn, this is what I get? From day one, I have told you that you are a killer, Leonardo! A killer of man, the murderer of the poor and rich, the thief of souls, and the monster of the devil!"

"If this is what you believe you have made me for, then you shall have what you asked for." Leonardo's eyes turned from light hazel to a deep red full of rage.

While Leonardo flew toward his maker, Boris stood in his place with great calm. It was until Leonardo had a grip around his neck that Boris grabbed hold of him and shoved him deep into the ground. He then picked Leonardo back up and threw him again into the collapsing house. It was unclear whether it was the speed of the vampire or if the townspeople began to lurk around from the commotion, but with the air filled with gas and Boris drenched from the liquid, flames of fire began to engulf the grounds. Boris was quite amused by the determination that Leonardo had gained. Then again, he did not want to kill him but wanted to teach him a lesson to never go against his maker.

Meanwhile, Alydia was nearing death once again. She watched the flames take over the walls that were once her home. The only thing she thought about was Leonardo and that all she wanted at that moment was to have him next to her.

Leonardo could sense Alydia's pain and wanted to end this now. He walked back in the direction of where Boris fell, and before he could strike again, Boris slammed him into the nearest wall and assaulted him with a metal rod that came from the collapsing house. Leonardo cried in agony as the rod hit him across the face and into his chest, barely missing his heart. Boris knew that his power and strength were more than Leonardo could bear. Without a care for caution, Boris walked by the rising flames and stood in place, waiting for Leonardo to take his turn.

"Still want to continue playing this foolish game?" Boris asked.

His attention abruptly turned to Alydia as she gave out a painful moan due to the blood that she was losing. "Maybe I should turn her and keep her as the daughter I never had. With her beauty and talent, I am sure she will make a better newborn than you ever would."

Boris's words hit Leonardo painfully in his heart. Finding all his strength, Leonardo clashed into Boris, taking them both through wall after wall, until the house finally began to crumble beneath them.

"She is mine!"

Flung into the ground, Boris and Leonardo were struggling to break apart from their anger. Quickly, without a second thought, Boris grabbed a broken piece of glass and stabbed it into Leonardo's back, this time inches away from his heart. Leonardo screamed in pain, for he felt the glass graze upon his cold heart. He could sense that he was reaching the end. He had failed himself and failed to keep Alydia safe. He was in despair for the first time in his vampire life. Finally letting his grip go of Boris, Leonardo began to drag himself to be at Alydia's side. But Boris knew better than to let him go to her so easily.

For his last lesson, Boris jumped onto Leonardo and bit him on his neck. He tore into Leonardo, tearing out a part of his neck. Leonardo yelled out in agony.

"It does not have to end this way, Leonardo. I can still save your life and hers. You both don't have to suffer this way," Boris said, coming up to his feet now, rejoicing in the victory that was his. "I can give you another chance to live forever. I only ask that you stay with me, learn from me, and let me teach you how to fully live your true life."

As the house began to disintegrate, Leonardo began to forget all his pain, anger, and any emotion that he felt toward Boris.

"I'd rather die than stay with you. You can remain in your own shadows of regret as you burn in hell for eternity!"

Using the last of his willpower, with great speed Leonardo came behind Boris and bit him right back in the neck. Boris was furious, and he bellowed in agony.

Remembrances now rose for Leonardo. He remembered everything and everyone. All the pain that he had afflicted on innocent people, the blood that he shed to make it thus far, and the hurt he caused his only family. Alydia, his sister, was alive. He was ashamed of wanting her for himself and going after her as a prize. The anguish filled up Leonardo, for he witnessed in the eyes of Boris the death of his family. Boris killed his family. He took away all that he had, and now he was on the verge of taking his life and his sister's life. He wouldn't let Boris get away with this. Leonardo wanted to know why he did what he did, but before he could ask, he heard Alydia's voice calling for him in pain. He slowly pulled the glass from his back, making him scream in anger. Every emotion he felt before came back to him, striking his cold heart, causing him to feel an inner power rising. In a brief moment, Leonardo furiously grabbed Boris and threw him out into the air, making him crash through the walls until Boris stumbled back into the earth, yards away from the house, briefly unconscious. He realized that he wasn't healing the way his vampire skin usually did, for he knew that his abilities were weakened by the amount of blood that he lost.

Getting through the pain, Leonardo made his way to his sister.

"Leonardo," Alydia said, her blood now covering the divan.

He stared into her eyes with such sadness and regret. "I never forgot you, Alydia … I never forgot," Leonardo said as he dropped to his knees next to her.

Hearing those words, Alydia knew that her little brother was back, and she began to cry. She felt that Leonardo always knew who she really was all this time, and all he was trying to do was protect her from Boris. While they reached out to hold each other's hands, they both looked into each other eyes and knew that they were family and that they loved each other very much. "I love you, my little brother. I …I always knew we would be together again," she said to as memories of young Leonardo came to her. From their happiness, it seemed as if time had stopped for them. They didn't care about the fires that were surrounding them or that their childhood home was crumbling to pieces; they knew nothing else mattered because they only cared that they had found each other after so many years. "God, take my soul! Damn it to hell if you must but let her live. Let her live her life through you!" Leonardo exclaimed. He leaned toward her, placing his forehead on hers, while Alydia shed her last tears and gasped her final breath.

Seconds later, the house fell on top of them. Both on the verge of death's door, they did not let go of each other but decided it was time to let go of life. Alydia died from her wounds and the flames that took her life. Leonardo cried out to the world, for he knew that she was gone. He couldn't save her. Alydia was the one person who truly cared about him. With great sorrow, Leonardo knew that he was unable to heal from Boris's attack and so decided willingly to let the flames consume him. As tears poured down his face, he was in frenzy for losing the one being who truly cared and loved him so much. He had lost the one good thing in his life. Forever.

As the flames continued to consume the land, the red-cloaked woman appeared from within the shadows of the woods. Having witnessed everything, tears filled her eyes, knowing that she couldn't interfere. All hope was now lost. "Good night, my prince," she said in a whisper. With a great weight on her shoulders, she went back to where she came from, swiftly disappearing into the darkness.

EPILOGUE

The life of Leonardo Le' Muerte was unique. His world was upturned by the massacre that Boris caused his entire family, for reasons unknown. Out of pity, Boris made him into a newborn, to cast him into a world of darkness and misery. He gave him a life that a human could never endure. The immortality and the internal dark gifts of a vampire, the beauty and seduction, and the pain that Leonardo learned and fought for—it was a curse that haunted him for all time. Unlike the other vampires out in the world, whether young, masters, or ancient, no vampire would ever forget to convey the chronicle of Vampire Leonardo. The vampire who loved, lost, and lived a short life as one of the most powerful newborns in the history of the Vampyr.

✻　✻　✻　✻

The following morning, the townspeople of Pittsburgh rushed to the scene. Entering the burned house, they found the ashen body of Alydia. For years to come, the massacre and the fire at the Le' Muerte house became the known landmark of the town. Generations told the story but a version of their own, for no one knew what really had happened that night. The only proof they had of a love that occurred during those last moments was a letter that Alydia kept deep in her pocket for her loved one to read at the timely moment. Somehow, mysteriously, it was barely touched by the flames that consumed the house.

October 8, 1789

To my loved ones,

If you are reading this letter, then I presume you already know what I have chosen to do. Since the murder of my family and especially the loss of my beloved brother, I have grown in a world full of hate and darkness. The life I had hoped for never came true. Michael, thank you for being the older brother that I never had and for understanding my reasons for doing what I have done. Simon, with all my heart, I thank you for being there to take care of me throughout all these years. I do not know where I would have been had I truly been alone in this world. I will always love you. Now I must go to find my brother because I know deep down he is still alive, and I pray that we will be together forever for all the days we missed. I will never give up until happiness and joy finally come to our family. To my loved ones, I bid you all farewell.

With love,
Alydia Le' Muerte

* * * *

The memories, the tales, the myths, and the chronicles of the lives of Alydia and the vampire Leonardo would never be forgotten for centuries to come. For the vampires that existed and were born anew recognized Leonardo's chronicle as "the vampire who chose love and death over immortality." Leonardo had proven as a newborn vampire, in a short period of time, that no matter what you become, you could choose to live by your own will and live an immortal life with happiness. This was the chronicle of *The Newborn*.

VAMPIRE LEONARDO

VAMPIRE BORIS

ALYDIA

THE SERIES OF THE ANCIENT
CHRONICLES WILL BE CONTINUED.

ACKNOWLEDGMENTS

I have to begin by thanking my amazing wife, Melody. She helped me every step of the way by editing drafts, giving me advice, and making sure every detail was accounted for. She played an important role in making sure that this book fulfilled everything I wanted this book to be. If it hadn't been for her, who knew if this book would ever have been published. Thank you for believing in me and for always being there. Thank you for all your love and support. Te amo, mi amor!

Nanita Ruiz and Ellie Rayo, a special thank you for contributing to the publishing of this book. Of everyone, you firmly believed in my work and demonstrated your support by believing in this book. Your friendship and support will forever be remembered, and I will always be grateful.

Ms. Carol Lewis, thank you for being one of the first people to assist me during my first draft of this book. You are a mentor to me, teaching me how to deliver impactful sentences and reminding to pay attention to the details. You are the best!

Thank you to Lulu Publishing, for allowing me to publish my book and to showcasing your great care during the process. I am deeply honored to have published my first book with your company. I could never be more grateful to make one of my dreams a reality. Thank you!

Last but certainly not least, I would like to thank my family, the Delgado family. You all have always supporting me in all of my crazy dreams and ideas. You have never failed me and are always there to love and cheer me on. Love you guys!

ABOUT THE AUTHOR

Richard A. Delgado is a full-time animation artist and part-time writer of fantasy novels. Born in Monterrey, Mexico, and raised in Houston, Texas, he now lives in Southern California with his wife. He holds a master's degree in visual development and is currently working on his second master's degree in illustration at the Academy of Arts University.